Rafael Has Pretty Eyes

Also by ELAINE McCLUSKEY

The Most Heartless Town in Canada

Hello, Sweetheart

Valery the Great

Going Fast

The Watermelon Social

Rafael has pretty eyes

stories

ELAINE McCLUSKEY

Edited by Bethany Gibson.
Cover and page design by Julie Scriver.
Cover image: *'imaged-fervour' O*, copyright © 2017, by Julie Whitenect, mixed media silkscreen on paper, 9×12 in., juliewhitenect.com
Printed in Canada by Friesens.
10 9 8 7 6 5 4 3 2 1

Library and Archives Canada Cataloguing in Publication

Title: Rafael has pretty eyes / Elaine McCluskey.
Names: McCluskey, Elaine, 1955- author.
Description: Short stories.
Identifiers: Canadiana (print) 20210288698 | Canadiana (ebook) 20210288736 | ISBN 9781773101637 (softcover) | ISBN 9781773101644 (EPUB)
Classification: LCC PS8625.C59 R34 2022 | DDC C813/.6—dc23

Goose Lane Editions acknowledges the generous support of the Government of Canada, the Canada Council for the Arts, and the Government of New Brunswick.

Goose Lane Editions
500 Beaverbrook Court, Suite 330
Fredericton, New Brunswick
CANADA E3B 5X4
gooselane.com

To the front-line workers who took care of us.

“Life is just one extended series of anecdotes strung together until they kill you.”

Contents

It's Never What You Think It Will Be

I am at a Toast 'n' Roast for my mother's fourth husband, Wayne. Wayne, of course, is a dud. Who else do you get on the fourth attempt: Idris Elba? I brought my roommate, Cedric, because I like having backup when dealing with my mother, the master of the emotional ambush. You never know when you arrive at a sushi bar for your thirtieth birthday if your new stepfather will be there holding a foil balloon. You never know if his name will be Scuffy or Dwayne.

The roast is at a Lions Club hall with shaky ceiling tiles and twenty tables dressed up like they are going someplace special. On the tables are programs, each with a photo of Wayne wearing the smug face of a reality TV polygamist. Outside it is winter in Canada and cold as hell.

"Imagine you lived someplace hot," says Cedric as we locate our table: unlucky #17. "Say, Mérida. And every day you could just get up, put on a T-shirt and *live*."

"Sounds sick," I admit, buying in.

"Is that what makes a Canadian," Cedric asks, "the ever-present fear of perishing?" He gives me *that* look, the one that tells me we are leaving the here and now. We are strapping on our what-if wings, and we could, if we tried hard enough, be MMA fighters or berserkers. We could be heroes. "Is that why we high-five each other when one of us defies those fears, when one of us does something batshit crazy like the dude in Alberta who decided to fight a cougar bare-handed to save his dog?"

"A cougar." I am impressed.

"Outside a Tims."

"I guess I'll just put down my double double and fight a two-hundred-pound wildcat known to kill animals four times its size. A predator that can jump twenty feet. I'll just fight *him*."

"Because I love my dog."

"Well, that's something, isn't it?"

"I had a girl and I thought she loved me but she didn't," says Cedric.

"How'd you know?"

"She slept with my brother."

"I had a girlfriend who only dated me because I owned a Newfoundland dog."

And then we both stare at the head table and I get *that* feeling—the one that convinces me that life is one inside joke after another and that people fall into two categories: the people who believe *Trailer Park Boys* is real and the ones who don't, and I no longer know where I fit because last night I saw Bubbles driving a Maserati Quattroporte with smoked windows on the Waverley Road in Dartmouth and it seemed quite normal to me. It seemed as normal as anything I am doing on this particular fucked-up day.

•

How bad can it be? I think. *This day? A day roughly one-third through my expected life—a life that has been both shitty and amazing. How bad can it be?*

The Lions hall seems harmless enough. Located in a modest area of squat vinyl houses and small businesses. Massage therapists and barbers. Marquee signs with changeable letters arranged into pithy messages: *Getting You Where It Hurts* and *PHD on Duty: Professional Hair Dresser.*

It took us twenty minutes to get here. Driving from downtown Dartmouth, where Cedric and I rent a three-bedroom flat in a two-storey house near a lake and a duck pond. It's a quiet enough area. Two blocks away is a group home for troubled youths—we call it The Escape Room. Some of the kids are okay and some are messed up on hard shit like heroin, and every couple of weeks we see cop cars and a group-home supervisor pointing up the sidewalk. Someone has escaped.

Our apartment is sweet, though, with a huge back deck and a BBQ. Trees all around us. Cedric calls it our Enchanted Forest. An older woman named Vera, who does eyelash extensions, lives downstairs. The tenants before us moved after twenty years when the outside stairs became too much.

When my Newfoundland dog turned three, he developed hip dysplasia, and I had to carry him up twenty-eight steps, a one-hundred-and-forty-pound dog that slobbered. I've done worse things in my life. At the time, I had a girlfriend named Lexi and she decorated the steps with white lights from Costco, and we drank craft beer until the stars came out. And none of it was real.

For a week I've been hearing squirrels in the attic, but Cedric says they aren't real either. It has become a thing between us: what is real and what isn't. I say, "We should do something about it," and Cedric says, "It's your imagination," and I say, "Squirrels will chew up your wiring," and he says, "That's an urban myth."

Two worn-out guitarists are providing background noise before the speeches start—*Musical Entertainment by Road Weary*, according to the program. One is wearing a fringed brown leather vest and an Oasis hairdo. Strumming "Take It Easy." They are the kind of guys who get murdered in a boarding house. *The parties were known to each other.* I admire their tenacity; I admire the fact that they are both half-cut and will, by the end of the night, be hammered.

"Hi, Michael. Hi, Cedric."

"Hi, Mom."

You told me that my sister would be here, but she isn't.

"Hello, Mrs. Sparling."

"It's Spinney, Cedric. Spinney."

My mother had taken the long route from the head table, to the very back where Cedric and I are seated with six strangers. It took her a while to find us. Table 17 is next to the washroom door, which keeps opening and closing. Old men keep coming out, still wiping their hands.

My mother is smiling but not looking at me or Cedric. She is scanning the room, seeing who might have noticed her in a sharp black dress, her hair just so. My mother sells real estate. In the summer she wears those sporty skirts with sleeveless golf shirts, a hat to keep the sun off her face.

I am here only as proof that my mother is not a failure, that four marriages were not a bad thing because "look how Michael turned out. He is an accountant, and that's his friend Cedric"—she glances at Cedric to make sure he is dressed "appropriately." He is, in a blue sports jacket and mustard-coloured straight-legged pants. I'm in a smart black dinner jacket. She lets us know that we have been inspected and will be again.

"Isn't it nice," she asks, "for Wayne?"

Ever since my mother married Wayne, she has been trying to convince me what an upgrade he is from Dwayne. Five-foot-four Dwayne was a plumbing contractor who drove a black behemoth decked out with chrome. Number Two, Blaine, was a retired helicopter pilot who had worked in Saudi Arabia and had hired five sex workers for his fiftieth birthday. I know all of this because my mother *told me*.

My mother has returned to the head table with Wayne, who wears a red boutonniere on his lapel. Wayne owns a cottage on the ocean, a party boat. He used to be in politics. The roast is supposed to be honouring him, but that, we have discovered, is a front. It is really a fundraiser for the elected Member of Parliament and his name is on the posters above Wayne's, thereby affiliating me and Cedric with a party we did not choose to be affiliated with.

The MP wears a one-way smile. He is that *that guy*. The guy who goes to funerals to be admired, who takes his son to dinner on his birthday and abandons him to work the room.

"Maybe we *should* go to Mexico," says Cedric.

"What about the book?" I ask.

"It will get done," he says in a tone I recognize. "It's under control."

Sure.

Cedric is a ridiculously talented artist. He is also bipolar. Sometimes Cedric decides to do sick things and I go along with him, thinking I am being a good friend. And then—after a $600 flight to LA to watch the turtle races at Brennan's Pub—he becomes depressed. The turtles, he decides, were boring. What we really should have done, he says, was to have saved our money and gone to Tokyo to see Doglegs, an outlaw pro-wrestling league, where the disabled fight the able-bodied because they aren't afraid of getting hurt—they have passed that point in life and are fighting in another dimension, and there is no reality, there is no script. That's what we should have done.

Cedric is supposed to be illustrating a children's book about a boy named Abdul, but he is painting watercolours of waves. When the editor calls, he tells her, "I am at my easel as we speak." After weeks of urgent emails, he agreed to meet her at Starbucks and deliver the Abdul art. He talked about waves. She told him she had bad luck with men. She was wearing a cute T-shirt that said *Be the Person Your Dog Thinks You Are*. They both laughed, and she left empty-handed.

The speeches have started and one of the roasters is telling jokes about Wayne's recent marriage.

"Why do men die before their wives?"

"Because they want to."

My mother should be embarrassed but she isn't.

There is a theory by a scientist named Dunbar who studied monkeys and it goes like this. Humans can really only have one hundred and fifty friends. Within that circle are ascending circles of intimacy: fifty people you could call "close," fifteen you could turn to for sympathy, and only five, just *five*, who are there no matter what, and some of those are family. How wrong can a theory based on monkeys be?

Most of the people in the room are what they euphemistically call "party workers." Smiling, glad-handing, jockeying for an appointment or a job. The vibe is so peculiar, so forced, that you feel like it is a cover and something shady is happening in the back room, and if you opened a door, you'd find a *Breaking Bad* meth lab or someone being baptized against their will.

These are the people who dress in party colours at conventions and jostle to have their picture taken with The Leader. They come in wheelchairs and straw hats. They bring the most frightening teenagers you will ever meet: Young Liberals, Young Conservatives, Young Henchmen and Data Miners of Tomorrow. This is them.

The family seated at table 1 exists only as proof that nobody gets everything in life — they are all doctors and lawyers, but they are profoundly unattractive, with huge brainiac heads shaped like marshmallows and W.C. Fields noses, mouths that flap open, exposing teeth covered with spittle.

The bar is the only thing real here, the only thing I like. It looks like any Lions Club bar on a Saturday night, with a man named Billy pouring five-dollar beers into brittle plastic glasses. Billy is wearing a white shirt he slept in. He has a wine glass for tips. He drives a 2002 Mercury Grand Marquis. He owns an aluminum boat for duck hunting.

"Do you think it can snow any more this year?" asks Cedric.

"It can *always* snow."

I don't mind the winters as much as Cedric. I'm a winter surfer, which is why I live in Dartmouth, a hop to Lawrencetown Beach near where I am going to build a house someday. I am used to strapping on stuff — a wetsuit and booties — in sub-zero temperatures, changing outside my car while my nuts freeze off. If I had my wits about me, I'd be home right now, looking at house plans. Five minutes after I agreed to this, I knew that it was one of those decisions that you impulsively, magnanimously make, telling yourself that you have been paranoid, too suspicious, in the past. And then it blows up in your face.

"Number 17," I tell Cedric. "You know what that means?"

"Bad luck if you are Italian?"

"It basically means, 'your life is over,' which could be true, or 'you are screwed,' which could also be true."

Cedric shrugs. "Story of my life."

The meal is a rip-off for the one hundred dollars they are charging—frozen supermarket chicken cordon bleu with a scoop of lukewarm potatoes and beat-to-death carrots. Would it have killed them to have sprung for a little gravy? I am actually embarrassed for the server, a friendly woman in her eighties.

There is one free glass of wine and I get Cedric's because he doesn't drink. When his meds aren't working right, he gets confused. Yesterday he convinced himself that he had left half a pizza in the fridge and the next morning it was gone. That and a litre of Coke. "Do you think the squirrels ate it?" I joked, but it wasn't a good joke, it wasn't a funny joke because he *was* confused.

Tonight Cedric has brought his Fujifilm X100F, which is small and sneaky as a squirrel. He is slyly shooting everything from a low angle, with close-ups of people throwing back their heads and garishly laughing. Wild cutaways to Road Weary, a tragicomedic duo. Cedric does that eye-lock thing with me that he does, that please-just-go-along-with-this look, equal parts conspiracy and begging.

Go ahead, I think. *Why would I care?*

Cedric collects scenes from all over the place and later decides what to do with them. Sometimes they end up in surreal shorts he posts online. One day Cedric came home with a guy he had filmed outside a bar: a weird old dude in full disco garb. A big disco hat, shiny platform bedazzled shoes, and LED light-up thingies on his fingers. On the video, the Disco Dude was staring into the camera and talking politics.

"Have you ever actually met a fascist?" asked Disco Dude. "I did, thirty years ago in Sydney Mines, and he was not what you would imagine. Yes, he was a fanatic, but he had the loveliest singing voice you have ever heard. He could—with three notes—make you cry."

The next roaster is a former politician.

Ten years ago, he was charged with sexual assault. He was acquitted after the party went to the victim's house with a cheque or a threat, depends on who you talk to. The rapist has a slide show: Wayne in a sombrero. Wayne being hit on the rear with a broom. Wayne dressed like Minnie Pearl. I can feel the smarm creeping into the room—a low-hanging fog that becomes progressively denser until all of our clothes are soaked with something that is neither rain nor snow.

Cedric and I went to a wax museum in California. We posed with Mike Tyson and it was uncanny valley. The figures were all so lifelike, so close to human, that they creeped us out, they made us think of death and question what it takes to be real. It's the same eerie feeling here—the roasters *almost* seem human.

Oh shit. One of the men at our table is choking on a piece of chicken gristle; he has covered his mouth with his napkin and his eyes are getting wider and wider. . . . *Now his face is red. Oh nooooo.* I am almost ready to get up and help him, when June, our octogenarian server, punches him crazy hard in the throat. *Thank you, June.*

When Cedric brought home Disco Dude, the dude said something I think about at times like this: "It's never what you think it will be. The End." You go through life convinced you're going to get diabetes like your old man and one day you choke to death on chicken gristle, and the autopsy shows your blood sugars were perfect.

•

I knew my sister wouldn't be here. I knew it. Some days, it feels unfair that I get roped into all my mother's dramas while my sister dodges them. But then I decide she can only handle so much. I love my sister; but she's different—she belongs to a swing dance group for starters. She has more exposed nerve endings than I do.

I'm an accountant so I am fairly bloodless. I drive a 1965 Buick Wildcat because it's ironic. I tell people my name is Micah not Michael. I'm the type of person who mocks events that could be painful, rendering them, or so I tell myself, powerless. Lexi and Todd—the guy she was secretly dating the whole time we were together—went to Paris last month and he spent every day making breathless Instagram posts.

The food, the sights! Todd gushed.

Who would have thought? I asked myself. *Nicer that Sierra Leone? Oh wow.*

Cedric and I played the substitute-a-word game. Every time Todd used *baguette* in a stupid post, we stupidly substituted *penis*. It made me feel better.

When in Paris, stuff yourself with coffee and penis. Everywhere you go, you see people with a penis in hand, just a piece of paper wrapped around the middle to protect it. Her cradling a penis; him gnawing on his penis like a Popsicle. The guy with the steel cart, wheeling brown paper bags overflowing with penis. The morning lineups for penis.

The next roaster has the same colouring as a red squirrel I saw on my deck. And he is awful. Him being in a position of power is more than dumb luck. It's a misalignment of the stars. It's the kind of phenomena that causes flash floods or tsunamis; it is nature's way of reminding man that we are powerless.

"Viagra is like Disneyland: a one-hour wait for a two-minute ride."

If everything is ridiculous, if everything is a farce, then it almost serves to negate the event, doesn't it? The awfulness of the night. That's what I tell myself. That's my mantra.

But I have stopped listening at this point; I am thinking.

About him. It was 8 p.m. when I saw him. An outlier on a bicycle. He was wearing a ball cap and drinking a McDonald's pop. Picture this: Small and in his twenties, wearing a plaid hooded jacket. The kind of guy who works night shifts as a dishwasher. He has a Budweiser cooler bag on his back. He's almost at the Halifax bridge and he's not driving for his health—he is going somewhere. About two hundred metres from the suspension bridge, the one that sad people jump off, the one that is supposed to be cursed, a siren goes off and the lights flash, and it's on. Away he goes. Straight across North Street. A split-second call. Through an opening in the median. Down the hill and under the bridge. And the cop car, which could have been chasing murderers instead, pulls a U-ey, lights screaming. Over a helmet violation. And when he vanishes from sight, legs pumping like hell, down low like a New York bike messenger, I hope he makes it. I hope we all do; that's what I hope.

Good Lord. What is going on? Another man at our table is choking. I kid you not. On a bun! A bun left over from the horrible dinner. And just like the other guy, he has covered his mouth with his napkin and his eyes are getting wider and wider. *Where is June?*

This time I am going to have to get up; I am going to have to punch him crazy hard in the throat, so I do.

My heart is pounding so badly that it might just explode. I am clearly not the dude who fought the cougar; I'm not cut out for this hero business. I am *not.*

The choking drama over, Cedric puts his camera down and casually checks his email. There is a frantic message from the author of the book he is illustrating. The bad-luck-with-men editor has informed her that Abdul has been cancelled because Cedric's artwork is not in. It's a big deal, it was already in the catalogue. He feels bad for the author. She's nice.

"She'll understand," I tell him, and he nods *maybe.*

*

The last person roasting Wayne is his mistress. She is a lifelong "party worker." One of those women who stayed at the bar too long. By the time she decided to leave, all of the catches were gone: married off to a nurse or a public prosecutor in a black suit. She's everyone's confidante. You would think she would be a femme fatale but she's not; she's a walking, talking snowman with a round torso and a round head, and a yellow bob instead of a felt hat.

In this room, everyone is disturbingly naked: there is no Facetune; there are no thinned noses and widened eyes. No turkey necks erased.

The mistress's speech is a titter of double entendres and inside jokes. Wayne rubs his tiny hands in amusement. The family with the gigantic marshmallow heads laughs, except for the matriarch, who is stern-faced and wearing pearls. A man from a free publication filled with snapshots pops up and takes the mistress's picture. Detached from the tawdriness of it all, the drunk guitarists with the Oasis hair *almost* look noble.

My mother stoically smiles.

And then—as though she has been in the next room the whole time, watching the farce on Livestream—my sister sends me a text.

Is it awful?

No. I reply. *It's fantastic.*

Do you remember when you were old enough to realize that life was not going to be perfect, that it wouldn't be all trips to the pool and Barney? I had that epiphany at my eighth birthday party, which I recall in a series of searing, disconnected scenes that pop into my head uninvited when I am driving to the beach and it is -20°C. The two "cool" boys from school didn't show. Some kid asked why my dad was drinking beer. And then my sister ate a peanut and she couldn't breathe, and my mom had to rush her to Emergency in a taxi, and my dad forgot to hand out the *DuckTales* treat bags. And that night he left and never came back. Up until that point, I thought everything was going to be great.

As we leave the hall, I hear the last fading bars of "Hotel California." It makes me think about the time that Cedric and I flew to California to watch the turtle races and then went to Muscle Beach and the Museum of Death, and he posted videos. And maybe it was my idea, not his. All of it. And maybe I'm the one with the dumb plans, not him. Maybe that's why I root for the outlier on the bicycle, just to mess things up, and maybe someday that will bite me on the ass.

But not today.

Today wasn't that bad, I tell myself, as we pull away from the hall. Not great. But not bad. All the way home, I tell myself the same thing: *it wasn't that bad*. Not nearly as bad as the day my dog died. Or the day I found out about Lexi and Todd. *Today was tolerable*, I decide. And it would have been if it had ended just then. At 10 p.m. on a snowy road before I saw four deer I mistook for lawn ornaments. After I tried to make Cedric feel better by lying and saying I ate his missing pizza. Before we came home and discovered he had been living in our attic for a week. Ever since he got kicked out of The Escape Room for siphoning gas and fighting. Brandon is his name. Remember that, will you? And he doesn't really want to hurt anyone, he tells his strung-out fucked-up self, but sometimes shit happens, and somehow he has a gun, and it *is* real, and all I can think of is Disco Dude saying, as though it had been written on a coffee mug, "It's never what you think it will be."

It's Your Money

Trevor is wiring $200 to his "girlfriend" in a small African country he will never, in this lifetime, see. He repeatedly asks during the Western Union transaction what the exchange rate is—down to the fifth decimal point—even though the currency he is dealing with is near worthless and the decimal point has as much impact as a sigh.

"Hmmm, so you say the rate is 0.012210, and the US rate is 1.32220?"

"Yes, Trevor."

"Hmmm. Well, last Tuesday it was 0.012213—"

"Last Tuesday I was in love."

"Hmmm."

Trevor has a shitstorm of papers in his shoulder bag, all covered with numbers and letters. Miraculously, from underneath the prescription pill bottles and the loose Jolly Rancher chewy candies coated with lint, he is able to produce the exact item he wants: cross-referenced US vs obscure African country exchange rates for the last fourteen days, the even numbers circled, 13 highlighted in yellow. If 13 occurs anywhere in today's rate, Trevor will not complete his order.

"Why, again, are you sending this money?" asks the man behind the bulletproof glass, a man who knows your bank balance, your vices, and your virtues. Your 2019 tax statement and your credit score. A man who has "Brian" embroidered in cursive gold on his black Your Money golf shirt.

"Because I have a very large fortune."

"Okay."

Trevor travels by bus, which in Halifax means you have given up all hope—you are either planning for the afterlife or believe you were cursed. Doomed to die during your next medical procedure or be audited by the CRA. You do not have to be anywhere at a precise time *or day*, and you do *not* have a very large fortune.

Trevor wears an orange reflective vest from a construction site, a wool hunting cap with earflaps like Charlie Brown's. He has type 2 diabetes. He weighs two hundred and sixty-four pounds, according to his bathroom scale, which he stepped on twelve times, removing his white socks and Costco eyeglasses with the holder chain, until the number was round. He has red dots on his face.

Trevor's apartment building is wedged between Good News Church and a home for women recently released from prison. It is a brick four-storey that has seen better days. One of his neighbours has a red dump truck parked in the driveway. He has convinced himself that Dailya will like it there.

The transaction complete, Trevor launches into a monologue, rattling off numbers and percentages, all the while ignoring one number: there is a zero per cent chance that Dailya, who is as beautiful as a beach with coral rag houses, exists, and will use the money to visit him in Nova Scotia at his ground-floor apartment that is infested with fleas.

"Okay, Trevor, we're really busy. You have to leave."

Trevor is used to people telling him to leave, so he goes outside to wait for his bus. He has a bag of Roast Chicken potato chips in his coat pocket, and he opens it.

Brian is two hours in to his shift at Your Money where he makes fifteen dollars an hour, which buys one bottle of Pinot Grigio poured into a Thermos under his desk. Brian is the lone worker on duty. Overhead cameras record him and the daily carnival of loaners, criminals, screw-ups, recidivists, and petty philanthropists, who could be divided into two groups: the people who have a plan and those who don't.

As bright and shiny as a showroom kitchen, the Your Money decor creates the illusion of respectability. The floors are beige ceramic tile, the walls off-white, the overhead lights recessed. The monochromatic colour scheme is calming. There is a row of six wickets, although only one—Brian's—is manned. Each has a stainless steel base and bulletproof glass to the ceiling. An FM radio station is playing.

If not for the Casino taxi idling outside—the same one that takes the alcoholics to the liquor store for their daily fix—one might think that the customers were doing okay.

It's Your Money!! Payday loans of up to $15,000. As required by law, there are signs explaining the exorbitant rates, but nobody reads them. *For unexpected expenses or covering a cash* *crunch, try our short-term loans. Western Union and Instant Tax Services, Friendly Cheque Cashing, and Currency Exchange.*

The phone rings and it's the wife of a Your Money loaner, which is what they are called. Not borrowers or debtors. Loaners. "Marcel will not be able to pay his payday loan," she explains in a voice that could best be described as strained, "because he is in jail for possession of child pornography."

"Totally understandable," Brian tells her, making a notation in Marcel's file.

When he gets off the phone, he Googles Marcel, and like approximately half the stories he hears, this one is true.

Brian has a black Fu Manchu, a honking nose, and he always wears shades regardless of the weather. As soon as he gets off he will don his electric-blue fedora, he will throw on his baggy grey hoodie and his beat-up leather jacket and look like he is ready for a night at a Montréal strip club or a pool hall named Sally's.

Eons ago, during the heyday of radio, Brian was a fast-talking, big-bucks radio host in Toronto. A "personality" who made prank phone calls to your mom and ran zany contests like Scavenger Hunt and Mystery Sound. *For fifty dollars, identify this sound.* He was Rockin' Randy, then Papa Bear, having more booze-and-coke-fuelled fun than any human since the days of Weimar Berlin. He had Maple Leafs seats. A white jacked Camaro.

Papa Bear's studio was decorated with Led Zeppelin posters and a photo from a bikini contest. Every day was an amped-up cause for celebration—there was National

Yo-Yo Day and National Chicken Wings Day, one running into the other.

When it all ended—the live remotes, the wrongful dismissal suit, the marriage—Brian did mellifluous voiceovers for a real estate channel on cable TV. *This lovely bungalow is open concept. It has all new stainless steel appliances*—

He drives a 1999 Chev Monte Carlo.

And halfway through the Thermos, all of this, his chaotic past, dulls to a soft roar. The loaners' jokes get funnier, the faces more friendly.

"My brother got the kidney failure," blurts a chronic overtalker, who is wearing a Batman T-shirt because he *could* be a superhero.

"There you go," says Brian.

Batman has those urgent eyes—the ones you cannot make contact with, the ones that are someplace else, starring in a different movie than you are in. He works forty hours a week in a warehouse but doesn't make enough to pay his bills and the more he talks the more he forgets where he is.

"He don't drink no water; he just smokes the wacky weed."

"Of course," says Brian, "because you can't do both."

It is an easy line—like telling Trevor that Dailya and her sister Zola are equally worthy and one would make as fine a wife as the other, and in some countries it is perfectly acceptable to have two wives.

•

According to its website, the average Your Money customer is your average Canadian: thirty-three years old, employed, with an annual income around the national average. The majority of Your Money customers have a traditional bank account "but prefer to use Your Money for (a) quick service, (b) convenient locations, or (c) non-traditional hours."

According to real life, the average Your Money customer is (a) hiding money from creditors or an ex-spouse, (b) getting paid under the table (contractors, tradesmen, mainly), (c) a problem gambler, (d) a drug dealer, (e) a one-timer with an actual emergency, or (f) just too stupid to know better.

Under *f*, you will find people who post bitter homilies online.

It is OK to Cut Family Members Out of Your Life.

Sometimes They Don't Deserve You.

They pay seventy-nine dollars for the three-hour Psychic Cruise through the Mist and the Mystical in Halifax Harbour and then become angry when the psychic tells them they will soon die.

•

"Good morning, Ian," says Brian, once known as the Voice of Gold.

Ian is a private dick who comes in from time to time with a twenty in the palm of his hand. He is looking for information.

"I'll let you know," says Brian, who probably won't.

Ian isn't the best private dick because he never lost his ex-Mountie arrogance, Brian has decided. He doesn't even try to be likeable. He still acts like it's just you and him, and he's been sent to your shitty trailer in the middle of horsefly-infested Nowhere because you sent a "threatening" email to someone in Veterans Affairs and he really doesn't like you and he has a gun.

"Anyone ever tell you that you look like Clay from *Sons of Anarchy*?" asks Brian.

"No."

Well, screw you.

At Your Money, you get both sides of the law.

The drug dealer Brian calls Lil Wayne.

Lil Wayne runs his whole business through prepaid Mastercards. In his late twenties, he is covered in tattoos —hands, face, neck—and he brings in $800+ in twenties and loads them onto his card, which does not require a credit check. He wears layered hoodies, some patterned, some plain. He will never get out of the business because he is clearly too messed up to do anything else—he will get shot in a warren of low-rental housing or arrested. Maybe both.

The louche lawyer Brian calls Charlie Sheen.

Charlie makes well over $120K but borrows $1,500 every two weeks and pays $330 in interest. Around forty, he has slicked-back hair and he wears suits with patterns: a faint check on the blue, bold white stripes on the grey. He could get his finances in order if he gave up the $300+

dinners at the dim restaurant with the charcuterie platter, but he won't—he will get divorced or suspended for "mishandling" a widow's estate. Probably both.

•

During transactions, Brian makes subtle controlled movements, as though he is minimizing his role in the process as well as the inflated interest rate. It is easy for Brian to keep a straight face because time has rearranged his features into a semi-permanent frown. The frown also shows that Brian is sorry, that he knows he was thoughtless and reckless, and no, some things are NOT funny.

Well, it could have been funny.

It should have been hilarious.

If only he had not picked Barry for the Scavenger Hunt. He should have gone with the sixth caller as promised on air. But Brian knew that Barry would be funnier, so he waited. Barry, whose stock expression when anything bad happened—whether it was someone falling off a roof or eating expired potato salad—was, "Ya can't fix stupid."

Barry had ginger hair and the most remarkable colouring—his skin looked so overlit, so bleached, that he could have been wearing a miner's helmet with an LED light. It was so unusual that Brian, when drinking, entertained the thought that Barry was an alien.

"Sorry Not Sorry" comes through the ceiling speakers and bounces off the off-white walls.

Sometimes it feels as though Brian has spent his whole existence inside a glass cage. Like the angry Customs agent at the airport or the poor devil collecting tolls at 2 a.m. on a forgotten highway to hell. Brian recently learned that caged animals can develop a form of psychosis dubbed "zoochosis" that causes them to harm themselves and hallucinate.

He also read a story that said lions, tigers, and bears in the wild are becoming nocturnal to avoid humans. He saw a coyote at night. Near the place he has his eye on, a modest Acadian house by the ocean surrounded by nothing but air. And you can breathe when you have air. You can walk from room to room if you want to. You can climb the eight interior wooden stairs because you have stairs to climb, and when you get to the second storey, there is air there too.

Your Money is in a strip mall between a denture clinic and a bagel store. Some customers enter with heads down like perps. George, eighty-two, strolls in as though he is meeting his buddies at Tims to talk hockey and tell tall tales. He wears a grey cardigan and Crocs and he has no serious money problems—he is just in the habit of loaning, in the same way that Trevor is in the habit of stockpiling plastic containers of watermelon-flavoured Kool-Aid when they go on sale for ninety-eight cents.

"So they got a new Canada food guide." George is a joker.

"That's a game changer," allows Brian.

"Oh yes, people will be rejoicing in the streets: 'Oh Doris, it's here, and it says hummus is acceptable as a meat alternative.'"

"Return that party pack of wieners!"

"When I was a boy, the teacher would ask what you had for supper, and you'da have to lie and say you got all your leafy vegetables. I never seen a fresh vegetable until I was sixteen."

"I thought arugula was an island in the Caribbean."

Brian and George laugh at their own jokes, and then George, his business completed, waits at the door for his son, who pulls up in a Ford truck with a front plate that says *Living the Dream.*

Last week on his day off, Brian drove two and a half hours to gaze at the house on the ocean. And then back again. On the highway, in a dead zone of asphalt and fir trees, he saw a rally for rich guys. Every few miles a rare car covered with stickers: a 1918 LaFrance with no doors or roof, two men strapped inside wearing white *Back to the Future* coveralls. A 1935 Auburn Speedster.

In front of him—just before he made his turnoff, the one that was part of his plan—was a red Karmann Ghia with a gigantic chrome-coloured key on the back, the kind of key you would see on a wind-up toy. The key was spinning round and round and it was the craziest thing.

At Brian's wicket is an older man, who reaches into his wallet and brings out three tens, his hand as steady as his faith in Jesus Our Lord.

"How you doing today, brother?" asks Raymond, who always calls Brian "brother."

"Excellent, Raymond, excellent."

Brian's voice is still sweet to the ear; when he says "excellent" it makes you want to rush out and buy something. It's not until Thermos number two, the backup, that things sound less sparkling, less posh.

"You ever get that mess cleaned up?"

"Yeah," Brian lies.

"Good. The Lord has your back, don't forget that, brother. When the devil is at your door, the Lord has your back."

Raymond hands out religious pamphlets that ask ARE YOU READY TO DIE? over a photograph of the Twin Towers blowing up. *Repent your sins*, the brochure implores. *Today could be your day.* Today all Raymond wants to do is send thirty dollars to Father Gamba in Zimbabwe so that he can keep his church programs in business. It's the same thing every two weeks — sometimes twenty, sometimes thirty.

Raymond used to be a courier, but he got fired for "aggressively" handing out *ARE YOU READY TO DIE?* pamphlets at a courthouse, an incident that made the TV news. Five years before that, his wife died of cancer.

"Anyone ever tell you that you look like Joe Frazier?" asks Brian.

Raymond laughs—it is a big open laugh, the kind of laugh you don't have time to think about, the kind of laugh Brian would like to get back some day. "No, brother, no, but I hope that Mr. Frazier is with Jesus."

Brian has been thinking about Frazier since the first time Raymond came in with twenty bucks for Father Gamba. Brian saw Frazier up close once at a fight in Montréal; Joe was with his sons. And he had that aura, the aura of someone who had done something big, something special. Smokin' Joe had a protean face: it could look happy one minute and sad as hell the next. Brian saw a photo of him once in a bad-ass black fedora, and his mouth was turned down and his dark eyes looked like they were watching a tragedy unfold. And Brian often wondered what he was thinking—was it the time he lost to Foreman or was it the Thrilla in Manila, that legendary death fight in which Ali tried to rattle him by calling him names? And Frazier, a sharecropper's son handsome enough to be in the movies, held a grudge for thirty hard years.

"The exchange rate today is 40.013," Brian tells a woman from the Philippines. Maria is part of a group of regulars— they all work two jobs and they all send all of the money from the second job back home. The women clearly have a plan.

"I come back," she tells Brian.

When the rate is not to her liking, she will wait. And apologize for taking Brian's time.

Most people in life want you and people like Maria to fail, and once you know that you shouldn't give a shit what they think. What you should do is this: hide your dreams, hide your hopes, hide your savings, in a place where they can't be hurt, where they can't be discovered. In a Morphsuit of secrecy. A cubicle of silence. That's what Brian thinks.

"Tuesday should be better," he tells her.

⁖

There are Your Money mysteries that Brian has yet to solve, mysteries as sly as life itself.

Jamie is a forty-seven-year-old property developer. He is not overweight but he has had two heart attacks because he lives in a self-constructed world of stress. Jamie routinely cashes cheques for $20K+. He says he goes to Your Money because the bank would hold the cheques if he cashed them there, which could be true or not.

Carl, forty-eight, is/was a freelance web designer with chronic foot infections. He had a decent income but he drove a junker. One day he cashed an inheritance cheque of $400K, paying the three per cent fee—$12K—when a bank would have cashed it for free. Six months later Carl's cousin ran a GoFundMe campaign for Carl's funeral.

Brian has been watching a show on Netflix about Jack Taylor, a hard-drinking, hard-living private investigator in Galway, Ireland. Kicked out of the Garda for slugging a politician, Jack still wears the blue peacoat. He swaggers past his mistakes and screw-ups. Brian likes the fact that Jack never saw a line he wouldn't cross—in one episode Jack goes to bed with his young assistant's mom and the assistant catches them.

When people say their lives were ruined by one random mistake they are usually lying. That DUI. Setting that rack of clothes on fire at Winners. Sleeping with someone's mom. If you do a forensic audit, you will usually find that the mistake is often the last in a series of very stupid mistakes. The one that went viral. Like Brian sending Barry the alien down a manhole and into an underground tunnel on the Scavenger Hunt, and Barry fracturing his leg and being trapped for fifty-two hours, triggering a massive rescue operation and a lawsuit. *Stupid, stupid Barry*....

Ian, the private dick, isn't Jack, a raspy-voiced rogue with his own moral compass. Ian reminds Brian of the officer who arrests a kid for having an open beer and then disables the interrogation-room cameras. Or the cop who gives an old lady a ticket for parking too far from the curb. Outside the hospital where her husband is dying. And now he is back.

Ian says the CRA has reason to believe that Maria is working under the table for a cleaning company at night. Brian has reason to believe that the CRA could, if it was not complicit, get its hands on the billions the well-connected stash offshore. And so he tells Ian that Maria has never wired money to anyone. "She's a loaner, a loaner."

And screw you.

•

Three days later.

Two rats are in from the sticks driving a filthy rat rod the colour of mud and dust, lowered and chopped and in your face. A beer jug for a windshield-washer container. The car is a manifestation of every anti-social thought they ever had; it is the middle finger on behalf of every working Joe who paid into a pension for thirty years and then got stiffed; and it is so profoundly stupid looking, so uselessly subversive, that Brian cannot help but think, *Good for you, buddy, good for you.*

Nothing in life is absolute; your wrong can be my right, and that truth is as old as love and death, envy and betrayal. That's what Brian thinks. Trevor can't come to Your Money anymore because they changed the bus route number from 12 to 13. Raymond got arrested outside a museum and made the news again, holding a sign that said, *ARE YOU READY TO DIE?* and in small print, *We are All God's Children.* He was wearing a blue sports jacket and a porkpie hat.

At that very moment, the museum was displaying an exhibit of human bodies from Germany. Someone's mother, brother, or daughter, their heart and skin and brain exposed for your prurient pleasure. Arranged in sporty poses: a latter-day Circle of Hell. All had been "plastinated" at the Institute for Plastination. And who even knew that such an institute existed, in the same country that conducted, not that terribly long ago, experiments on twins, by a graduate of the Institute for Hereditary Biology and Racial Hygiene? Mengele.

"I know you are doing your job, brother," Raymond had told the cop, his dark eyes looking as though they were watching a tragedy unfold, "but so am I."

Today Raymond tells Brian that he had a dream and Brian was in it. He was wearing a sombrero and laughing like there was no such thing as yesterday. Brian says he does own a sombrero and it has magical powers. It can make people taller; it can transport them through time. Raymond says that's a damn fine thing, and Brian, for the first time in a long time, smiles.

Hope

Morton looked younger than his years, and it was a trait that had both freed him and trapped him. It freed him to wear thin cotton T-shirts and to drift from one ethereal woman to another. It trapped him in that egoism most of us grow out of when we are no longer defined by our travels or our hair.

Morton had been my friend for a dozen years, and he was still as lanky as a high school basketball player. His hair was surfer-blond. Morton had a trademark red shirt and a trademark red jacket. When he turned thirty, he bought an old East Coast house, which he shared with a cast of roommates who did tai chi and wore burgundy pants.

When people saw Morton in a family photo at Christmas, hovering like a rare bird blown off course, they wondered if the whole thing was an illusion. He bore no resemblance to his bald, bearded brothers. Or his Costco-obsessed dad. His mom was blond and she must have carried tall lean genes; there must have been an uncle somewhere who looked like Rutger Hauer.

Morton showed up at the weddings of beautiful people. Some called themselves "creatives" or "marketing consultants" or "food writers." Less vague were the yoga instructors and baristas. Everyone seemed to have a solid supply of kombucha, guitars, and fine hats. White cotton shirts and suspenders. Rolled-up pants. There was always the odd lawyer and appliance repairman, and it was hard to tell one from the other.

All of this would have been fine, all of this would have been soft-lit, gauzy, and clever, if it hadn't been for Hope. Morton had no business at all being with Hope.

In hindsight, I can see things more clearly, the story of Morton and Hope and me. Things weren't going that well for me at the time. I was trying to make a living as a stand-up comic, stealing half of my jokes from Reddit. I did a *Game of Thrones* set one night, and it was brutal. I did another on handicapped parking–spot vigilantes, and that bombed.

When things are not going well, when you smell like flop sweat, you hate everyone. You hate them for having health benefits and a car, you hate them for posting photos of Machu Picchu, you hate them for being beautiful, you hate them for being ugly. Morton was my friend but I was secretly starting to hate him. I was secretly hoping that something bad would happen to him, which, in the end, it did.

The first time I met Hope was in a coffee shop with Morton. I made a joke and she laughed. And it wasn't even a fake laugh; it was out before she had time to fake it.

Hope was long-legged. She had rough red hair, which she secured in a ponytail that could never be blasé. Hope's hair could never pose insouciantly in rubber boots and coveralls. Hope had no more control over her hair than she did over the condition she had lived with since the age of two, the one that doctors kept in check until they couldn't.

Hope worked as an editor at a small publisher, she explained on that first day, the one that led to eighty-eight others. She had a master's degree and the lofty dream of being a writer, normally enough to make me hate her.

One day recently, I asked myself: "Did you *not* hate Hope because she was dying?"

"Well, that's a shitty thing to say," myself said back.

"I take that as a yes."

Hope was not even Morton's type, not from his ethereal template. Those women, all fine-boned with flower-child hair, were interchangeable and could be found in Instagram photos of Morton jumping into a waterfall, his white butt flashing. They wore bathing suits or slip dresses that fell off their frames.

Hope told us that she liked her job. She liked making scenes line up like dominoes. She liked the rhythm and rhyme of a perfect sentence. The gut punch of a visceral truth. Hope was obsessed with avoiding the superficial, believing that everything good, salient, and worth preserving lived below it. Below the obvious. I liked the way she said that.

Hope had written a novel, she said, but it swam across the surface of life without getting its face wet.

"How come?" asked Morton, *as though he cared.*

"The experts say you should write about what you are afraid of," Hope said. "Easy for them. Maybe they are afraid of snakes or clowns. What if I am afraid of dying, and writing about it could anger the gods enough to make it happen?"

"Okay—"

"So I write about doppelgängers and rabbits. I am stuck in the shallow end because I cannot swim. Metaphorically speaking."

"I will teach you how to swim," promised Morton, and I don't know if he thought she was being literal, if she *actually* could not swim.

"Will you?" she asked. "Will you?"

•

In the short time I knew Hope, here are the things I learned: children's authors are lovely but often bonkers, poets are insecure (and often bonkers), illustrators make magic but spoil the illusion by obsessing over details, novelists are hungry for validation, and retired PhDs are awful.

"Some of them are entitled despots used to having lesser people format their endnotes," Hope explained. "One retired prof announced that he would not be edited by a 'young nothing' like me."

"So, it's just one guy?" asked Morton.

I think Morton wanted to be a better person, less shallow. But there were pathways in his brain that he fell into; they were established long ago, the first time someone noticed he looked different. Taller, blonder, more youthful.

"It is never one guy."

Hope was droll and quick and she knew things. She was the type of person who would sleep outside your bedroom door if you were too messed up to be alone; she would stay there until you were safe. Hope would never tell your secrets. Or use them against you. And somehow, she met Morton.

Someone is always less jaded, less worldly than others; Hope was always going to go through life with the wind on her face and the sun in her eyes, and that shouldn't be a bad thing, should it?

Morton had been hired by a public relations firm of hip young people selected for the optimal mix of height, hair, and ethnicity. Like a Benetton ad only poorly paid. He was always telling me about the place. Everyone felt lucky to have been chosen, and so they volunteered at charity events on weekends. They stayed late. All were as photogenic as Morton, although some a full decade younger. While his new colleagues had been in college, Morton had been travelling to Third World countries on contracts with CIDA or NGOs, documenting relief programs in photos and words. Morton, he was told by Gwen in a job interview that never confirmed if he was hired or not, "brings something different, ahhmm, and we like different."

I saw Morton after that interview, and he wondered exactly what Gwen meant by "different."

"I am sure it was a good thing," I said, hoping it wasn't.

"I don't know," said Morton. "She was hard to read."

"You know what's hard to read?" I countered, trying out a gag. "Cats' eyes! I was in a staring contest with a Siamese for three hours and I still don't know what he was thinking."

Morton laughed as he always did.

After Morton was officially hired, I met Gwen by chance. I was with Morton at the farmers' market. Gwen was an extremely thin, extremely high-strung woman with glassy eyes. A runner. That day she was wearing Lululemon. It was not unusual, Morton told me, for Gwen to send you a work email at 10 p.m. It was not unusual for her to develop a sudden dislike for someone, whose life would then become unbearable.

Morton was unfamiliar with the nuances of office life: Who bought the coffee pods? Where did the banana peels go? First World problems.

He had no problem, however, working in a female-dominated milieu because he was an ally of women. If you look at his Instagram, you will see the post: "My growth has been promoted by female lovers, companions, and best friends. I couldn't possibly begin to tag all of you here."

Morton said it was a forward workplace. There was a room for meditation, although no one had time to use it. Morton's co-workers were open about their mental health, and he was understanding. He told me that a co-worker named Taylor cornered him in the lunchroom. She told him that one day her hand went through a window by accident and at first she thought she was okay. Then she saw the torrent of blood and she passed out. When she came to, she was disoriented, as if she had just been born with no knowledge of anything around her. She might have been real, she might have been dead.

"Now imagine if those three minutes of disorder were your life, and instead of lasting three minutes, they lasted three years," Taylor told him.

"Oh, wow," Morton had replied. "That is brave of you to say."

Morton was always telling people they were brave, including Hope, who had no choice in the matter really.

I see myself as an observational comic, but nothing was happening in my life. Nothing I could mine. I wasn't about to make jokes about the fact that Hope was dying.

Hope's parents were both dead, so were her two siblings. She was the first person I knew who had no one. She came from a moribund town with a cosmetology school set up in an old Stedmans store. From the street you could see the Styrofoam heads, you could see the workstations. *Find Your Future At Majestic Styling.*

I tried to imagine what it would be like to not have that phone number. The one that had not changed in thirty years. The phone number of a person who, no matter how maddening, how frustrating, loved you without an asterisk. And would come. Would take your side no matter how badly you had failed, even if you were "wasting" two perfectly good degrees like I was.

Whenever strangers learned of Hope's medical condition, she told us, they invariably panicked and said, "It could be worse." Before they blurted out an irrelevant story about a second cousin who had been born without ears or hit by a train —

"Or eaten by a gator while walking her cockapoo," I added.

Morton laughed.

If Morton had a redeeming quality, it was this: he would laugh at anything. He couldn't even help it. I would say something only remotely funny and he would explode with laughter. His teeth so white and happy. And if I said something that didn't work, I could see him trying not to laugh at the fact that it was so unfunny, and I liked that. I liked it so much that I went places with him and Hope just to get those laughs.

One day the three of us went for lunch at a sushi bar. Hope said that last New Year's Day she ended up in a Swiss Chalet alone. At the next table was a sixty-something woman and her weathered dad, a working man who had worn his very best sports jacket. They ate quietly and the daughter told him his jacket looked nice. The compliment meant more to the daughter than it did to him, Hope said, and the pair seemed to know that. He finished his pie. He was the kind of man, she said, who would never ask for much, and Hope was happy that the two were together. Happy and sad.

"I love you," said Morton, without a hint of shame.

"Do you?" asked Hope. "Do you?"

At the time Morton told Hope he loved her, she lived below a couple that were always having ridiculous roaring arguments that crashed through the ceiling. She had told me about them, thinking, I suppose, that I was looking for material.

I heard the couple arguing twice when I was at Hope's apartment, and they *were* ridiculous. They were as ridiculous as any act I had ever written. They were as ridiculous as the pants I wore at my last show, the "vintage" plaid polyester ones that made my ass look as big as a billboard.

The couple didn't seem to have any real problems—homelessness, unemployment, or a fatal medical condition—so they fixated on the petty. One night they were in a shouting match because the man had marched in a demonstration, waving a sign that said *I Love Scientists.*

"Do you know any scientists," the woman demanded, "or are we dealing in the abstract?"

"I know *some.*"

"Who?"

Long pause.

"Maybe none personally, but that doesn't preclude me from having an opinion."

"I have an opinion on Paris Fashion Week but it's worthless."

"Not the same."

"You know that my brother Craig actually is a scientist, right? He has a PhD in genetics. And last week he shot a seagull in my nana's yard and ate it. He called it 'foraging.' When I was in high school he ordered radioactive material from China and hid it next to my computer monitor, and I sat by it for nine months."

"That is anecdotal."

"My father had it tested—"

"Anecdotal!"

"Life is anecdotal. Life is just one extended series of anecdotes strung together until they kill you."

"I don't know where you are going with this."

•

Morton's new office was "dog friendly," he informed me. The animals were always underfoot, although some could not be there at the same time as the others so notice had to be given. Most were fine, but not Gwen's dog, Jeff. Nobody liked Jeff.

Jeff would bark ferociously any time a man entered the office. He broke a door. He smelled terrible. If Jeff ate something bad he would vomit or crap on the floor. He was forever in the garbage, and someone got in trouble because Jeff scrounged a banana peel and Gwen said, "Those are not good for him."

"If you truly believe that your dog is a *person*," Taylor riffed after the banana incident, "ask yourself, 'how many people bring their ninety-year-old nanas to work?'"

Would you like a treat, Nana?

She threw up last night, so don't give her any more treats.

Sorry, Nana, no treats for you.

Sad face.

Oh no, Nana had an "accident!"

And then they all laughed, including Morton, who thought I would find that whole scene funny.

Hope had some elaborate theories, like the one about family portraits. The ones you see in photographers' display windows. They were, she was convinced, a jinx, a lightning rod for heartbreak and tragedy—the kind of heartbreak that changes your internal wiring and molecular structure, the heartbreak that leaves you altered. In some of the photos the children are toddlers. In others, teens. Everyone is dressed in all-white or in matching plaid, leaping into the air on a sandy beach or posing in front of a blue bokeh backdrop with the family dog. Bathed in a strobe light of wholesomeness. So that the mom, after a tough day at work, after riding a rancid bus, standing next to a man with a massive backpack, could look at that photo and tell herself she had done something right. Hadn't she? She could have the photo blown up, framed, and placed over the couch. She could make it her Facebook display photo. And what did she really know? Hope asked. What did she *really* know when the call came from the hospital or the police station at 3 a.m.?

And that's how a life changes, Hope stated. A perfectly acceptable life with celebrations for birthdays and anniversaries, a life of hockey tournaments and Boston Pizza. A life that had, until that night, been just fine.

I nodded knowingly, and Morton, although it wasn't the right time for it, laughed.

In the lunchroom of Morton's office there was a fridge and on the fridge magnetic Scrabble letters. It was the custom of the office to arrange them into the words to suit events that were unfolding—Xmas, Campaign, Moving—and then one day someone arranged them into Shitty and Dog and Vomit.

There were always secrets hiding in plain sight, Morton said, secrets that consumed an inordinate amount of office energy, and if you weren't in on the secret, you were screwed. And if you didn't know there was a secret, the others assumed you were in on something. There was an uncool IT guy—he and his friends called each other edgelords—and Morton was sure he wasn't in on any secrets. During a party, the IT guy made an observation and instead of responding with "that's interesting," everyone stayed dead silent.

"It was awkward," Morton told me, "epically awkward."

Morton's office was a curious mix of the callous and the childlike, he said. One minute someone would be mocking the edgelord's stutter, and the next they would be gushing over a fatuous piece about Hogwarts house fashion tips. He never knew, he told me, who his co-workers really were.

Hope and Morton and I went to Lunenburg to visit one of Morton's ex-girlfriends, a clever woman who designed clever hats. Inspired by time in Peru, she made women's bowlers. A red felt hat called a montera that could be filled with flowers. Tall white hats.

All of the houses in Lunenburg, home of the *Bluenose* schooner, were painted ribald colours. I was thinking of moving, I told myself, although I wasn't sure if I believed it. What if I moved away from my so-called career and everything that defined me? What if I became a new me? We went to a Tim Hortons, and at the counter were two boat-building apprentices and they looked content, as though their days were laid out like the plans of a schooner. They were wearing steel-toed boots and plaid shirts with traces of sawdust. Black toques. They looked wholesome.

Hope carried a notebook and she wrote something down for her next book. You could tell Hope was an impatient person by the scars on the back of her hand; in too much of a hurry to reach for an oven mitt, she often grabbed a useless dishcloth. Hope didn't own a car, but she walked at high speed as if she was trying to get to her parking meter before it ran out.

I never did figure out Morton's angle with Hope, why he had plucked her from the display case of available women and added her to his virtual charm bracelet. Hope was more *my* type than his, I told myself. Hope and I saw things that Morton was too self-absorbed to see. I hated the fact that Hope had fallen for Morton's shallow charm when I could not, even if I tried, be that shallow *or* charming.

Hope told us that she once had a neighbour named Buzzy and he was a character. He had worked out West, and when he was young he was with the circus. And one day, he felt sick so he went to Emergency, and they took him into the examining room, and he never came out. Cancer, stage-four by then. And pretty soon, they stopped giving him water, they cut off the IV, they upped the morphine, and two days later, he was gone. And he died alone.

"You won't," said Morton.

"Okay," said Hope. "Okay."

One night, Hope texted me—she couldn't reach Morton. She had been in the hospital, this stay longer than the others. And now, barely home, she had received a message from one of her children's-book authors, who was on a street sobbing. Paralyzed with emotion. The author, who had written a book about a blind boy who could fly, had been out for a walk and had seen a husky lying on a lawn, a purple light flashing around its neck, *on off on off on off.* The big dog eerily motionless. Flat on its stomach.

The author had been there for twenty minutes. She needed to know if the dog was alive, but she was afraid of the people in the house—they had wrecked cars in the driveway, an 81 Hells Angels sign in a window. There were shadows.

"I'm so sorry," she kept sobbing. "I'm so sorry but I can't leave him—"

By the time Hope and I arrived, the author had cried herself into stillness. We put her in my CarShare vehicle, circled the block, and, just as we returned, the big dog with the flashing light twitched.

I drove Hope home, and she invited me in for a beer. The upstairs couple was having one of their ridiculous arguments. I never did get to see them, but I imagined that the man looked like Seth Rogen if he had not made it in Hollywood.

"Are you the devil?" the woman demanded. "Are you?"

"Stop this crazy talk," the man replied flat-voiced.

"That's where you go when you are painted into a corner of deceit, onto a ledge of dishonesty. You go to the 'crazy talk.'"

Silence.

"Well?"

"Well, what?"

"ARE you the devil?"

Silence.

"Yes, I am the devil. I am Satan, Lucifer, Beelzebub, Iblis. That's me. The one who brought death into the world. Yes."

"As though it is something to be proud of!"

Silence.

"Are you proud of it?"

"Yes, I am extremely proud of being a force of evil."

"I am not surprised."

I looked at Hope and said, "There are worse things than being alone."

And Hope the orphan said, "Are there?"

•

Some people are created to be warnings for you—orange pylons on the highway of life. They are the worst version of you and sometimes that makes you change your ways. Give up drugs, stop posting bathroom selfies. An old soccer buddy of mine OD'd in a seedy hotel in Cambodia; a cousin found religion and joined a group that tried to convert LGBTQIA+ folk.

Morton, Hope, and I went to a wedding of gauze-lit beautiful people. Hope and Morton a couple, me their dateless friend. And after the *lhasang*, Morton did it right under Hope's nose. The way he always does it when he decides it's time to drift from one lovely woman to another.

"You are not a very nice person, are you?" Morton chirped at a willowy brunette passing by with a mimosa.

"What do you mean?" she asked coyly, intrigued by Morton who, of course, looked tall, blond, and youthful in his white cotton shirt.

"A nice person wouldn't walk right by me."

"I don't *know* you."

"Right."

"No, I *don't know you*."

"Oh damn, you aren't Sam, are you? I thought you were Sam from animation at the art college."

As if there was a Sam, *as if* such a person existed.

"No, I am Jasmine from Duncans Cove."

"Okay," Morton smiled. "Can we just forget about Sam?"

A giant laugh and then they were inseparable.

Hope and I took a taxi home from the wedding, and we barely spoke. I wanted to say, *Don't take this personally*, but how else could she take it? She had just been personally replaced. When you have erased all the rough edges, when you have buffed your persona to a youthful glow, you have no traction in life, and that was Morton. He was a set of summer tires, and he wasn't equipped for the storms and blizzards of the heart; he was never going to pull you out of a catastrophic ditch. Morton could be brutal.

So here is the part where things went south for Morton, the failure I was secretly hoping for. He described the whole thing to me, although he still wasn't sure exactly what had happened. He'd been "framed," he told me, sounding like a character in an old movie.

"Who are you?" I asked, "Roger Rabbit?"

Despite himself, he laughed.

Gwen had summoned Morton to her office at 4 p.m. on a Friday. A bad sign. Taylor put her head down when he walked by her desk, which made him nervous. Those things always go down that quickly, Morton said, that invisibly, all of the pieces assembled under your nose while you see nothing.

Morton was barely in a chair —

"We are, ahhmm, letting you go today," said Gwen.

"Really?"

So awkward, I thought…

It started to get vague after that, Morton recalled, shock muting the words and their meaning. There was something about the company accountant and a severance package for Morton and three never-before-seen disciplinary letters in his file. And then Morton saw the headlights of the train, but it was all too late.

Someone is always more clever, more duplicitous than you. Gwen was always going to go through life with the meter running, calculating how much someone was worth to her and when it might be wise to dump them on the side of the road, and that shouldn't be a good thing, should it? That said, Morton kind of had it coming; he *had* been mean to Hope.

Morton was being fired for "bad performance," Gwen said, but only because the firm did not want to go to the police with the more serious issue. The criminal one.

"The police?" said Morton, confused.

"We could still pursue that."

This is killer, I thought.

"We've consulted our lawyers."

Morton said he went silent because he was trying to keep his balance, he was trying not to fall off the merry-go-round that started up at full speed before he had a chance to grab a bar.

Someone, Gwen said, had been poisoning Jeff the dog in slow and steady increments, leaving the unspecified poison in the garbage can in the lunchroom, the one that smelly Jeff was known to "visit." And it was "an enormously serious problem, ahhmm, a serious *crime* actually.

Jeff was at the vet for over a week, ahhmm, there is a chance that he could have died."

"Died?"

This was comic gold.

"That is NOT, of course, ahhmm, why we are letting you go, but—"

Morton didn't hear the rest, just, "It changes things."

So yes, I admit, I felt better when that happened to Morton. Does that make me a bad friend? Clearly.

After a couple of days, we went for beers. Morton said he didn't care if Jeff had been poisoned or not. Cold, I said. He told me that he had already lined up a contract to photograph an orphanage in India for disabled children—the photos would be used by a non-profit organization fighting poverty, vulnerability, and physical weakness. He said Hope was a sweet girl, but the timing was off. Yes, it was too bad that she was dying. And what about Jasmine? I asked. Who? he replied.

And then for some reason—curiosity, boredom, vanity—we decided to do something random. We both submitted our DNA to an online genealogy site. Knowing Morton, I am certain he expected his results to show that he was descended from Vikings or a Swedish king, people who were handsome and virile.

Three weeks later, the results came back. Morton was informed that his forebears were from Belarus and Turkey, and shortly after he decided to enter "a period of self-reflection and listening." He left early for India, booking into a yoga retreat.

My results were far more outstanding. There was a match with my not-so-confidential DNA sample and three unsolved murders, which meant one of two things: either I was a serial killer or someone related to me was. The victims were all ex-cons, one body was still missing. Who were we: the Sopranos? The police were on the case. It was just a matter of time before they contacted my parents to tell them about our murderous connection. My father wouldn't care—he is *that* bored with life—but my mother would be beside herself. My mother who has, as you may have guessed, a family portrait on her wall.

This was amazing, I thought. I felt relieved that something bizarre, something solid, had finally happened. I could use it in my act. I could make it funny. *Mom, you're not planning on digging up the garden this year, are you?* Stuff like that. *Boy, that rose bush has really taken off. What kind of fertilizer are you using?* I had two brothers—one was an apprentice sous-chef—I could work him into the bit. I could see the mirth meter rising.

But first I wanted to tell Hope, who was still my friend. I had already imagined the conversation. As my story came together, my timing bang on, all of the elements lining up for the perfect arc, she would squint and say, *That's so cool.* And then she would smile like she was proud of me.

But I never had that chance because a miracle happened. Hope got *that* call. The transplant call, and she went to Toronto just like that. Gone, as though Morton and I had never existed. And the weird part is: it was such an epic thing, such a colossal thing—bigger than the fact that I still hated people who owned cars, bigger than Morton and his trip to India, bigger than smelly Jeff, bigger than the fact that I was *totally* related to a serial killer—that everything else seemed small.

This was life and death, the only thing we all had in common.

And there was probably something funny in there.

Let It Go

It is 2:30 a.m. and Big Boy says he is not leaving until he gets a fight.

He's thirty-five and wearing three hundred pounds like he owns an all-you-can-eat Italian buffet. He used to bounce in another bar, so he knows some of the staff. Tonight he is just a customer but he has it in his fat head that he has to have a fight. You know how you get something in your head—like your cat has superpowers or you really can play drums like Dave Lombardo, Godfather of the Double Bass.

"C'mon, man, just go home." The Hub bouncers are too beat for this. You can see it on their puffy faces, as clear as the sign that says *Shoes must be worn at all times.*

"No, I wanna fight."

Big Boy works as a sheet metal installer. That day after his shift he had spent three hours powering through *Resident Evil 1* live on Twitch. Now, he is just sour drunk and stupid. He could be banging on the door of an ex's apartment, he could be arguing that "Georges St-Pierre should *only* fight at one-seventy—"

On and on it goes until he pushes a supervisor; a bouncer puts him a chokehold and takes him to the floor.

Hard. A bar stool goes with him. That's how it always happens. *That fast.* Holding him by the limbs like he's a stag that's been shot, it takes four bouncers to carry him out. His face is red with blood, and the bouncers know, they just *know*, it is going to be on their clothes.

The whole thing is unnecessary, the bar staff think. He's not *that* dumb, he's not *that* high. He is not Rambo, the delusional joke on MDMA who claims he is Special Forces and after his girlfriend is arrested, phones the cop shop around the corner: "I am walking there now. I am former JTF2. You have one hour to release her." He is not the mouthy girl who gets kicked out for not wearing shoes—"You can't enforce it; it's not written down." You just knew she would get arrested and then yell at the cops, "My man's in jail. I know my rights!"

Big Boy's girlfriend is sitting on the curb crying because she tried to make him leave twenty minutes ago. Before this *had* to happen. A hairstylist, she has Popsicle-pink hair. Last month, it was violet. "Dannn-eee," she sobs.

Ten minutes later, she will still be there, still crying.

Everyone looks like a celebrity mug shot at 3 a.m.—the makeup is worn off, the night's expectations dashed. It's your bad side, and the flash of disappointment makes your skin look greasy and the edges of your face too sharp.

By now the street sounds as sad as a break-up story. It is emptying, leaving clean-up to the paid duty cops like Mack, who is regularly under investigation for excessive force. Mack got in trouble last year for roughing up a kid, then forcing the kid's friend to delete footage of it.

"Keep walking, String Bean," he orders a lanky dude lingering too long, "before I string you out on the ground."

The Hub boss comes outside as Mack is putting the cuffs on Big Boy.

"What the fuck is your problem, Danny?" demands the boss.

Big Boy replies, in a monotone of stupid, "Well, I deserved that."

Mack cuffs Big Boy too tight and whispers something the bouncers do not hear. In a black goatee and a navy blue ball cap, Mack looks like he is wearing a disguise. Last year, he appeared in a public service announcement of cops doing push-ups for suicide prevention, appearing deceptively normal unlike the cop from bike patrol who looks like he's a white supremacist but isn't.

Under Mack's ball cap is the first clue — an aggressive, black, razor-faded pompadour. Under his left sleeve is the second clue — a long, ugly scar.

Mack classifies civilians by three categories: assholes, whack jobs, and innocents. Assholes are the tall-ship crewmen from Italy who grope women and carry roofies. "You come to Italy, cop, I fuck you."

Whack jobs include the law student in the blue plaid shirt, who tells a pretty bartender named Gina that he murdered someone in a drug deal but, "They'll never find the body."

It is as though they believe that nothing they say at night is permanent, that it will not be exposed the following morning — on a sticky sweat-and-beer-and-piss-soaked floor — next to the wallets, Fitbits, and condoms. The broken glass and the EpiPen. Like it somehow doesn't count.

Innocents are people like the special needs teen whose father drives him by the bar three times a night. They come to a near stop, so that the teen can wave to the outside bouncers. And the bouncers, who like him, wave back.

For the past six months Mack has been on a collision course with someone, and no one knows who that is going to be. You know how you get something in your head: like you really cannot stand the face of that ginger barista with the Hitler youth haircut and the waxed handlebar moustache. Mack has something in his head and he can't let it go no matter how hard he tries.

"Oh shit," curses a bouncer. "I got bit. Do I need a shot?"

"Yes. That idiot could be carrying Ebola."

"Hoof and mouth disease."

The bouncer who got bitten by Big Boy is named Will and he's back on the door two nights later. Will moved outside three months ago for the extra dollar an hour. He checks IDs, does pat-downs for drugs and weapons, mostly knives these days. "Sorry bud, you are far too drunk," he says far too often. Every incoherent falling-down drunk who gets refused entry is suddenly a lawyer or a law student who "knows my rights."

They come in packs: twenty-somethings with cleavage and tight T-shirts smelling of Marc Jacobs's Daisy or beer. Some of the cute girls wear little black dresses. There are the outliers: the older swinger couple who bring their date. The TV host in his on-air-ready suit, who pretends that he is on a phone call until he gets to the front of the line and tells his imaginary phone friend, "Okay, see you inside."

Outside may have been the wrong decision Will now thinks. It rains and snows too much, and he always feels sick. One night it rained so hard that the grass cried and the trees whimpered.

Will looks like a football wide receiver at a small Canadian university, which he was until the third concussion. Six foot one and built, he bounces three nights a week to cover rent. He has perfect teeth and azure eyes. Will used to date a nursing student named Lissa who owned a rabbit named Peter, but they broke up; she said Will had become "moody." He's not so sure about that.

Will's family lives an hour away in a village that has an agricultural fair and a beauty pageant, a white wooden church where he made his First Communion. A covered bridge. Biblical floods that occur on random years when the ice breaks on the river, basements drown, and horses cling to the high ground. *Get a Kit*, the government tells you. *Make a Plan.*

Will hasn't told his mother that he bounces; she thinks he works after school at Costco stocking shelves. If she did know, she would just lie awake waiting for him to text *home* at 3 a.m. Will is at that stage where he is fighting to escape his mom, escaping long enough to try to be who he wants to be before he returns to who he is.

Moms like his wear their hearts on their sleeves. They start out believing that none of life's tragedies will visit their families if they avoid their parents' mistakes, and that's just false. There is no direct correlation between how hard you try and how kind the gods will be to your children. Someone will still develop mental illness; someone will still get sexually assaulted at a swimming pool. The mom will blame herself.

Will's mom doesn't know that he wakes up with headaches or that he has trouble concentrating in class. Some days, he swears he sees double. She doesn't know that he drove himself to Emergency after Big Boy bit him.

At 9 p.m., she had sent a text: *Hope you had a good day at school.*

He had texted back: *It was great. Just getting a pizza with Lissa.*

Love you xoxo

Love you, too. xoxo

You can't predict the things that get under people's skin. One of the bartenders, a lifer in his fifties, had a son in sports, and he spent every nickel he had on that kid. In the end the boy missed the Big Show by a blink, and it was something the bartender could not let go. He could *not* let it go.

"Your boy at the Olympics yet?" someone would ask, and Randy would launch into a painful monologue about a rigged set of trials.

"Aww, that's too bad."

Randy knows everyone by name, including two shop-worn habitués who occupy the brass bar. They look like

Statler and Waldorf (the grumpy old guys) from *The Muppet Show*. Almost spitting images. Statler, the taller, more genial one, wears a grey suit and brings the young female bartenders Laura Secord chocolates.

Randy and Statler invariably go through the same ritual.

"What can I getcha?" Randy asks.

And Statler collects himself and furrows his brow: "What craft beer do you have on tap?" He tries to make the query seem important; he tries to make himself sound discerning—a beer snob, an aficionado, someone who cares about hops and malts—when in fact he just wants a drink.

"Your son hear back from the fire department?" Statler asks.

"Naw, not yet."

"Those things take time."

And then Randy goes off about a "dumb-ass" story that had been on CBC about "some douche" who competed in a masters competition in his son's sport. "The dirty fuckers never wrote a word about my boy when he could have used a hand, when he was trying to get sponsors so he could stay in the sport—"

"I hear you."

"Masters is pay to play," Randy keeps saying, "pay to play."

Statler, a retired lawyer with a condo in Boca Raton, isn't listening anymore. But he nods.

The bar could be in Anyplace, Canada — it could be Halifax, it could be Thunder Bay; it is a warehouse of hope and wanton distraction, and hope feels the same whether there are dartboards on the walls or mauve neon lights on the ceiling. Camo ball caps or barmaids in Oktoberfest dirndls.

The next Thursday night is an international shitshow.

A troupe of Australian male strippers named Thunder from Down Under show up. They are still wearing bronzer and open white shirts. They smell like coconut and weed.

Around midnight, one of them is getting kicked out for fighting, but he won't comply. It turns into a scuffle. The bronzed stripper resists so violently that he ends up with a dislocated shoulder. He is outside crying and swearing. One of the cops grabs him from behind to settle him down, he flips out, and the Thunder from Down Under manager yells, "Brett, calm down, it's the coppers."

Mack is not on duty. He's always tired lately, he told one of the other cops. "It's those lights," he explained. The city recently installed LED street lights outside his house, and it's that *Seinfeld* episode with Kramer and the Kenny Rogers chicken sign — so bright it's like daytime. He hung blankets on his windows, but it doesn't help, so he is always tired.

During the day, Mack and the other cops are real cops with guns and bulletproof vests. In Mack's place tonight is an old cop. He looks like Scruff McGruff, the cartoon crime dog in the trench coat, the one in the anti-weed video that warned kids: "Never try marijuana... don't try it at all... it's like banging your head on a wall... it is doing you no good at all." He's been a year away from retirement for years now.

McGruff is tight with a pimp named Marco who tells him the bar next door is slack on pat-downs: "I got friends who go in every night with guns." McGruff tells Marco that you never know about people, *you just never know.* He was on a flight out West to see his daughter, and the guy in the seat next to him was a real-life flat-Earther, the first he ever met. He was a lapsed Mennonite from Manitoba who "awoke" in 2014, he said. "So you never know."

Scruff McGruff doesn't do much of anything and then occasionally snaps and arrests people who are simply annoying.

Will is telling a kid he can't come in because he is wearing fake NBA basketball shorts. Dress code. No shorts, no track pants. One night, he denied entry to two Russians in red Adidas warm-up suits and they acted stunned, as though they had stepped off a plane in Sydney, Cape Breton, instead of Sydney, Australia: "What?"

About forty minutes later, the kid returns, puffed he is wearing jeans.

"Where did you get those?"

"Traded them with a hobo for twenty bucks."

About an hour later, the bouncers see Stevie, "the hobo" who is HIV positive and a heroin addict. He has open wounds that he scratches. Stevie is wearing fake NBA basketball shorts, and by the end of the night, he will be back in his second-hand jeans, which are stained with piss and blood.

One of the bouncers asks Will about Emergency.

"Ten hours."

"Waited fifteen once."

"They want me to come back on Monday," he blurts.

All Will wants to do is finish school and get a job at a physio clinic where he can lead people through their exercises and maybe go to a Patriots game someday.

"For the bite?"

"Yeah, I guess."

Sometimes, two SWAT cops sit across from the bar in their car to keep an eye on things. One night in winter, they saw a punk throwing snowballs at Will. The handsome SWAT cop, the one who looked like he was from IMDb, told the punk, "Stop trying to act tough, June bug. If you don't stop, you're going to jail."

All the cops are antsy about the fentanyl. Two milligrams is enough to kill the average adult, and it is showing up in coke and in fake prescription drugs. Cops found pills containing fentanyl stamped as OxyContin, Percocet, and Xanax. Everybody's antsy.

It is the movie star cop that Gina, the pretty waitress, decides to talk to after she saw a story on the news. The one about the body at the bottom of a pond. She tells the cop about the law student in the plaid shirt who laid out the story of his life at 2 a.m. How he mentioned the murder as though it was just another detail to get out of the way. After the fact that he was in law school and had played hockey in the QMJHL. Before the fact that he'd grown up on a farm. "I thought he was lying," she said. "Now I think it's true."

A man in his thirties gets kicked out for being high on blow. He is talking crazy talk. "I will not leave until you release me from the premises." It sounds like he watched a YouTube video of sovereign citizens. Talking about his person and how they were required to release his person. The bouncers tell him to get lost; he says he is calling "the authorities." Will looks over and the dude has Google searched "911" instead of dialling it, and on his phone is a photo of the Twin Towers.

Twenty minutes later, an old woman arrives in a Ford Fiesta to pick the dude up. You can tell they have done this before. She looks like the saddest mom Will has ever seen. When you've been to hell and back, you are different. Stiller, smaller, less effusive. You have lost a layer of yourself that will never be replaced—it's been scorched off, torn away like a boat cover left out in a storm, and the you that remains is alive but less. Just less.

The mom drives through a stop sign without slowing down.

Mack likes moonlighting. By the time you get home *that* time has passed—those interminable hours when you lie awake thinking, that time of doubts and second guesses. It has passed. And when you are on the job, there is always shit going down and you can't think too hard when shit is going down. You just can't. Like when a team of JTF2s goes crazy, fighting everyone in the bar. You arrest them, and one of them hands you a card with a number, and you call, and the voice on the other end instructs you, "This needs to completely go away. None of this ever happened." Like a Matt Damon movie.

•

Earlier that day, Randy the bartender buried his cat in his backyard. Under a scrubby birch tree. And he cried his eyes out. The family adopted that cat when his son got a bad break in his sport, and the ornery cat became a symbol. An orange fuck you. Randy had taken the long way home from the vet, his dead friend in the passenger's seat in his pink plastic carrying case. He couldn't stop thinking about how Rocky had no say in the matter. How it was left to Randy to decide. Live or die? And who was he? A stupid old man who had counted on a cat to stay the same, and he *did*, through all the ups and downs. That cat never changed; he didn't lock himself up in his apartment and refuse to speak to anyone "for wasting my life on that bullshit sport." He stayed the same. An orange fuck you.

•

McGruff had two days off, and he and his wife went to Nova Scotia. They drove to Digby Neck, forty kilometres down a sparsely populated road until they came to the end:

a seven-dollar car ferry that would take them to another world. To an island with brightly painted houses and fishing boats. Whale-watching tours. The Bay of Fundy tide was depressingly low as they waited for the hourly ferry—they could see mud and barnacles, they could smell rot. McGruff felt at the bottom of something: a geological formation, a life plan that was clearly, at that moment, not going to work out. They could no more escape to that island—where people were, at that very moment, throwing horseshoes outside a community hall, people whose families had lived there for two hundred years—than they could buy a loft in New York City. And he knew that.

An ex-con shows up drunk and insults everyone but Will. "I respect you, man." He is even bad-mouthing Big Tom who works at the bar next door, the one with guns. Big Tom is a six-four powerlifter whose pectoral muscle exploded during a competition. "Tom is a scrawny little piece of shit," the drunk charges. "My son is bigger than Tom." The bouncers tell him to get lost. "I wouldn't treat you this bad if you were in the pen," he slurs, "so you shouldn't treat me this bad." Eventually he goes next door, where he tries to push his way past Big Tom, who two-hands him.

It is 1 a.m. and it's raining and Will doesn't want to be here, but he doesn't know where he should be. Somewhere else, that's all. Somewhere. He tries to pin down one thought, to hold it still long enough for it to take shape, but he can't, and his mind feels like an awful Reddit thread that will not stop.

Nine p.m. *Hope you had a nice day. Love you xoxo*

Will hasn't answered his mom but he will tomorrow, he tells himself, when he figures out what to say. *Anaplastic astrocytoma.* The specialist had used the proper medical name for it, and that was decent of her, wasn't it? It gave Will time to collect himself and do a Google search on his phone. *Yeah, that's what it means*, but he didn't need to hear that right then, did he? In a sterile room with no place to hide his fears, no place to conceal the shock that had muted everything but his pounding deafening heart. *Anaplastic astrocytoma?* It could have been the name of an exotic flower that his mom entered at the agricultural fair, his mom who secretly checked her laptop at 3 a.m. waiting for his green Facebook chat light to come on, her signal that he is home.

He thinks about texting Lissa, but he doesn't. The Internet said there could be a cure.

Three months ago, in the nadir of winter when the rivers were imprisoned in ice, two mutts stumbled up to the bar. One had dyed white hair and a pig nose. Whitey worked at Wal-Mart but he thought he was hard. His friend lunged at a bouncer, so the staff took him down. Whitey jumped on a bouncer's back like a monkey, and Will pinned his face in the snow until the cops took over. Whitey and his friend got barred, joining a list of one thousand other losers.

Tonight he is back. Will tells him he is not allowed in, and he goes nuts. "That cray, man! That cray!" He won't let it go. He is cursing and kicking a metal box that holds free newspapers, making far more trouble than he is worth. *Clang.* "Fuck this." *Clang.* "Fuckin' pigs." *Clang.* He is wearing a thick gunmetal chain-link necklace that cost twelve dollars.

Scruff McGruff does this thing where he stands with his hands folded on his stomach, a calculated move that shows, in a pool hall of homicidal bikers, that he isn't scared. In a courtroom, that he is an honest officer who would never plant prints. Right now, as the night hits an apogee of stupid, his hands are in his pockets. There is an uneasy pause, a stop in the action that makes people question what they are doing. Whitey calls a pregnant tattoo artist in the lineup a "sketcher bitch," and at that moment his pig nose and his white hair are so annoying that Scruff McGruff tases him in front of eighty patrons waiting to have a really good time. And it happens so fast that you can't get your phone out.

Little Green Men

Shag Harbour, Nova Scotia, is two hours and forty-five highway minutes from Halifax, eighteen hours from Toronto, *and* 4,800 interplanetary hours from the red planet Mars.

There is no irrefutable evidence that they *were* Martians, but we do know—we positively know—that on October 4, 1967, something odd, something aberrant, happened in a small fishing village on the South Shore of Nova Scotia, something that people with an understanding of the sea and the sky knew was not right.

That's it. That's *all* we know. Me and you, that is. And the five hundred or so people of Shag Harbour, who have for over half a century, had this great cosmic mystery hanging over their heads like an unpaid tax bill.

Canada's Most Researched UFO Sighting.

The World's Only Government-Documented UFO Crash.

Investigated, studied, and if you believe the conspiracy theorists, covered up in a Cold War operation as elaborate as Roswell.

•

There was something odd about him, too. The stranger. Yes, he was from away. People could tell that by the red polo, the shorts, and the taupe leather sandals. But so was the math teacher at the high school—*she* was from away—and the Mountie with the black Lab. Him, too. And the American who drove up in June to the place with the weathered cedar shingles. The stranger's name was Chuck, but no one knew that. And yes, he did have *that* way of talking like they all do, fake sociable one minute and as sharp as a raised elbow the next—"How much did you pay for your boat?" But it wasn't just that.

The day he arrived, the fog was thick enough to shroud house numbers and signs, tragedy and joy. It was the kind of fog that when it rolls in from the Atlantic—an overlay of grey—bothers some people and provides others with relief. You aren't supposed to do much when the fog is that thick. You can just be.

People noticed things. The van was a rental, a black Chevy Express with no side windows. The man checked into a "chalet" in nearby Barrington Passage, Lobster Capital of Canada. He ate at the Pizza Delight. He went to the bread bar three times, and the third time, when he passed the couple in the adjacent booth, the boyfriend twitched, the way people who have been in jail twitch.

The stranger drove across a causeway to Cape Sable Island, where they have fish plants and a beach named The Hawk with a drowned forest, and at Christmas a tree built of lobster traps in honour of those lost at sea. It was three hours before he came back. What was he doing?

*

The next morning, Chuck got a coffee at Tim Hortons. "That your new truck?"—a server was flirting with a customer in grey baseball pants—and then he continued out of Barrington Passage. He slowed to let a mud-covered quad cross the road. "Free Fallin'" was playing on the classic rock radio.

After fifteen minutes, he eased into Shag Harbour and parked behind the only vehicle in the museum parking lot, a red Dodge Charger. The air tasted of salt. Across the street was a sign for the Guiding Light Baptist Church. It was mid-September, but there were hordes of mosquitoes in the air.

The museum was a slight yellow building, roughly three minutes from where it happened. If you drive too quickly, you will miss the sign. *UFO Sighting, 1967, Shag Harbour Incident Centre* is written over a sketch of two people pointing at a spaceship while three oversized cormorants, or shags, look on. Nearby are stand-alone signs shaped like Little Green Men.

It wasn't something to be taken lightly. The thought of aliens hiding in your fishing boat. Abducting your children. What if they weren't tiny creatures with pear-shaped heads and slits for mouths? Telepathic powers. What if they looked, people must have then feared, like you and me? Had people found themselves glancing over their shoulders, bolting their doors? Had they eyed every interloper with suspicion and wondered, "How do we know anything if we don't know this?" How long does that uneasiness stay with a place? All of it.

Chuck walked inside, paid his two-dollar admission, and admired the Little Green Man a student had built as a school project. He read the yellowed newspaper clippings. The *Halifax Chronicle-Herald* headline: "Could be Something Concrete in Shag Harbour UFO—RCAF." He watched the video that played to ten empty wooden chairs, the one that used words such as *otherworldly, thick yellow foam, creatures, military divers, a cylinder, NORAD, and British commandoes.* The same words used in the books and films.

And then he returned to the man at the counter, a gravel-voiced man whose photo was on the wall as a seventeen-year-old. Who had been on his way home from a dance on Cape Sable Island that night. *It was fortuitous,* Chuck thought, *that he was here. Him of all people.*

"Has it been busy?" Chuck casually asked.

"Not really," said Laurie Wickens, a senior in a ball cap, jeans, and a plaid shirt, who like most people his age, bore scant resemblance to his teenage self. "You would think the government would put up signs but they won't."

"Yeah, it is hard to spot."

"We had some Americans in and they said we should be getting thousands and thousands a year. Said we should be bigger than Roswell since that was disproved."

Roswell, New Mexico, where the American government had allegedly hidden aliens in 1947.

The two men shot the breeze, and then Chuck asked

the question he had been waiting to ask for decades: "What do *you* think it was?"

And Laurie, the president of the Shag Harbour UFO Incident Society, the first person to make it to a pay phone on that moonless night of October 4, 1967, at about 11:25 p.m., a man who initially thought an airplane had crashed into the ocean, a man who may have answered that very question a thousand times, said, "Your guess is as good as mine."

On his way back to the chalet, Chuck passed a car wash attached to a store that sold hunting licences. He picked up a sub sandwich at Sobeys.

You have to promise not to tell. As though he had a choice.

People know what you are thinking, Chuck told himself. If you put on a forced smile and pretend to be interested in their job, they know if you are judging their car, their family, their clothes. The beat-up Ford Escort with *27* painted on the side, the cyclist riding a bike with one hand, the other one holding an open Keith's. While Chuck was reminding himself to be careful, a conversation was replaying in his head.

"You know what we are going to do?" his wife had said, insistent. "We are going to drive across America and we are going to stop in those towns we saw in the movies: the movies with Jimmy Stewart or Kevin Costner. We are going to see them for real. And we'll drive across those arid stretches they used for westerns, and we'll see them, too. Maybe we'll end up in California—"

"We'll need a good car," he had said.

"We could take Route 66 and stay in one of those old motels—the Blue Swallow or the RoadRunner—"

"We'll need to buy a tent. And we *have* to have a reliable car. I am not driving across America in a Chevy Volt."

"We could drive through Pennsylvania where they made *The Deer Hunter*—"

"And break down in the middle of nowhere? What would we do then?"

"I don't care."

"Well, I do."

*

The chalet had a faint musty smell, like a hunting camp or an attic where you hid old love letters in a box. Chuck liked the feeling of benign neglect and otherness. He stared at himself in the bathroom mirror, which due to an invisible warp, made his face look gaunt. He liked that, too.

The first night he thought about how his wife slept with the window open, with a thick blanket on their bed holding her down like a pair of gentle hands. And yes, they could have been driving across America, escaping into old movies and iconic sights. But he was here instead, in a utility room with two beds separated by a wall that reminded you of divorce. Why? If anyone asked, he was going to say he was a professor writing a paper on how the UFO incident had impacted the residents of Shag Harbour; he was going to say he was from UBC because it was far away. But nobody asked.

•

On Sunday morning, Chuck drove half an hour to a former military base outside Shelburne, a Loyalist town that had played Puritan New England in a movie. When a producer made *The Book of Negroes*, the town got to play itself.

The derelict base was easy to find. When he exited his van, it was so quiet that the grasshoppers seemed amplified, like the uneven syncopated rhythm of a Harley at midnight. Discarded Tims cups were the only signs of life. A chain-link fence with barbed wire half-heartedly enclosed the once-top-secret operation, but Chuck walked right past the guardhouse with smashed-out windows. He walked right in. As the silence echoed in his ears—that silence that makes you feel as though the world has stopped, the silence that makes you uncomfortably aware of the sound of your own heart and breath—he passed two brick buildings. He stopped dead, thinking he had heard someone, but it was nothing.

Chuck could have been a government inspector, he could have been a travelling salesman killing time. Back on the top of the hill overlooking the base, he climbed inside the remnants of a cement bunker. He saw empty Monster cans, a cigarette pack, and graffiti. He took photos of a sign for a business that had once tried to repurpose the site: *Seacoast Film Production Studios. Welcome Aboard.* He shot the ocean.

None of this—the sign or the collapsing bunkers—was in the original story, the one that only he had heard. The one his father had told him, their secret, the thing that separated them from the others.

It was not their only secret. From the time Chuck was a child, his father had told him stories he was not allowed to share. He was always afraid that his mother would catch them, catch his father telling him secrets, and he would be in trouble. And yet his father kept doing it.

Chuck stopped at the Shelburne Tim Hortons. It was packed with people fresh from church, mainly seniors, but also a peculiar couple in their thirties—a mousey woman and a flamboyant little man intent on putting on a show.

"I would like an extra-large tea with two bags," the showman told the teenager behind the counter, "And make sure," he added lewdly, "that you squeeze my bags."

The server did not react, so the showman asked the teen if he had any Fruit Explosion muffins, somehow making the muffin sound lewd. The stone-faced teen dutifully went out back in search of the Fruit Explosion, and when he returned the little man had changed his mind. Once at his table, the man knelt on the seat so that he could talk to people in the lineup behind him. Every time he said something outlandish, the mousey woman tsk-tsked, "And you just came from church."

"She is studying to be a minister," he told one of the seniors who nodded approval. The showman was making such a scene that no one really noticed the stranger with the aviators and the iPad. He slipped right through.

Chuck understood why some of the stories had to be secret. His father told him about the time that he bet fifty dollars at the racetrack and won five hundred, and that seemed like a good thing to keep from his mother. He told Chuck that his father—Chuck's grandfather—had killed a man in the war and had to sleep next to the body. Maybe that was man talk. His uncle had robbed two banks in Winnipeg on Valentine's Day. But some of the secrets were puzzling, like the one about the base where he had been stationed as a diver. Why would his mother not know about that?

The next day, Chuck located another of the UFO witnesses. The man, now in his eighties, took Chuck to a work shed behind his house "away from the wife." It wasn't that cold, but the man was wearing layers of plaid, all blues and greys. He was dressed like he could be called upon to check a mooring or fix an engine at any time, and he'd be ready.

Yes, the old fisherman said, people knew all about the base in Shelburne. And yes, it was supposed to be hush-hush. But fishermen knew about the microphones planted at the bottom of the ocean to pick up Russian subs. It was the fishermen's job to know. They knew as surely as scientists now know that Mars is nothing but dry rocks and sand, that its atmosphere is 96 per cent carbon dioxide, 1.93 per cent argon, 1.89 nitrogen, with traces of oxygen. Is that all, Chuck wondered, that anyone knew?

*

The chalet had internet, and that night Chuck went online, and he found stories about the museum, conspiracy theories. Believers and non-believers. He found a travel piece by a snide outsider who wrote, "One of the worst museums you'll ever visit tells one of the most unusual stories you'll ever hear." There's a word for people like that but you'll only hear it over a game of 45s. People here will give you the benefit of the doubt until you prove them wrong, and then that's it. There is no going back. You will be always *that* person. Maybe it comes from going to sea where one bad call, one soft decision, can kill you and your crew of four, like those poor young men on the *Miss Ally* who died longlining for halibut in a winter storm. Chuck poured himself a drink.

*

On the third night, Chuck thought about his chat with Laurie Wickens, whose call, followed by others, triggered a five-day search by boats and divers, including Chuck's father. Chuck parsed each sentence, as though he had missed something the first time. Laurie told him that the two girls who had been with him and his friend the night of the dance had since passed.

"Was it foggy?"

"No," said Laurie, a retired fisherman. "Clear as a bell."

Pause.

"No full moon, no streetlights, but clear."

After five full decades, Laurie knew no more than that.

Outside the chalet walls at 4 a.m., there was nothing but that dark rural silence, muting the fact that things were happening all around—important things, like men getting out of bed and pulling on boots, and women already counting the days until their return, mothers praying.

In Chuck's family, their mother had been the judge of right and wrong, the arbiter of all disputes. "Go ask your mother," was the chorus of his life. She was the one who decided what school you would attend and what activities you would be involved in. Who was a success and who was a disappointment. Chuck was never sure why his father had divested all of his parental power in her—maybe he was away too much or maybe he had made an unpardonable mistake that showed he could not be trusted. Maybe she knew about the Valentine's Day bank robber. Whatever the reason, Chuck's mother was in charge, and all his father did, when he was home tuning up his motorcycle or cleaning his Winchester, was tell him secrets. "Knowledge is power if you keep it to yourself," Chuck had once written in a Campfire notebook he hid under his bed. His father's words originally, but now Chuck wondered: were they *true*?

The Mounties: they were the meat of the matter for some. It was one thing for locals, who could be written off as drunk or hysterical or pranksters, to have seen something that night, but three Mounties saw something too. Three men in red. Whatever it was, illuminated and sixty feet long streaking across the sky with a whistling sound and a *whoosh* before it crashed into the water, floated, and then vanished—we are told—without a trace. The foamy slick was described by witnesses as a "giant snail trail" with a foul smell "like burnt sulphur." Chuck tried to find the Mounties, but they were not to be found.

*

There were three boys and one girl in Chuck's family. Chuck was the oldest; the two middle children were typical middle children, half taken for granted.

From the time they were small, Tony, the youngest, was their mother's favourite. He was not the smartest, the kindest, or the most athletic, but he was the favourite. One year, the mother decided that Tony, an uninspired athlete, should get brand new goalie equipment, including special skates, when the other boys got hand-me-downs. When Tony was sixteen, she paid for a trip to New York City. Determined to maintain his status, Tony well into his forties, lied to their mother about everything, and she willingly, hopefully believed him.

"Tony was the top salesman last month," she told Chuck, days after his father's funeral, days before he had taken a flight to Halifax.

"That's great."

Tony's only claim to fame was that he had been on a TV consumer program testifying that his wife had lost $300 when she signed up for a free trial of skin cream. ("There was NO mention of having to send the samples back.")

The two middle children had moved to Alberta and rarely figured into their mother's stories. Just Tony.

Some of Tony's lies involved his children, two unremarkable teens.

"Tony says that Josh is going to be an astronaut," his mother told Chuck.

"Really?" asked Chuck, a commercial pilot.

"Oh yes, Tony says that is what he is going to do. He's decided."

"That's nice."

"They make a lot of money, those astronauts." She looked both pleased and proud.

"Yep."

"Does Nathan know what he is going to do?"

"Ahhh, no. He is still figuring it out."

"Well, Josh has decided."

Chuck was okay with the lying—who didn't lie to a parent?—but then he discovered that Tony was, to maintain his status, feeding his mother stories about Chuck's sons.

"Did Nathan have a motorcycle accident?" she asked.

"Well, yes, but it was no big deal."

"Was it his fault?"

"Yes. No. How did you hear about this?"

"You told me, didn't you?" she lied.

"No, I didn't."

The next day Chuck looked at houses along the highway. Most were modest—but every now and then, he thought, *That guy has everything the way he wants it. Not the way society says it has to be but the way he wants it.* He had a workshop, a boat, and a duck pond. A pair of matching ATVs and a jacked-up black truck to carry them. A ride-on mower. A miniature windmill.

He imagined that the owner was a man he had seen in the local Tims with his wife, a tall man with white hair a little too long in the back. He had a moustache and inside his short-sleeved cotton shirt, a thick gold chain. A man who knew who he was.

Chuck drove to Baccaro Point where there was an unmanned coastal radar station, another player in the Cold War. He saw a lighthouse, benches for people who wanted to lose themselves by gazing at the ocean, and a fenced-in structure that reminded him of a massive PEZ dispenser—a white dome on top of a four-sided metal base. He took, for posterity, a photo.

Some of his father's stories, like the one about what he had seen in the dark waters three hundred metres off Shag Harbour, were exciting. Who wouldn't want to know what it was? A disc-shaped Russian weapon? A meteorite? An alien spaceship? Chuck's father also told him there had been an accident once and one of his dive team had died, and he wasn't allowed to talk about that either. "Don't tell your mother I told you." And Chuck was terrified that his mother would find out.

Chuck thought about phoning his wife and then changed his mind. He had a bottle of tequila and he thought about drinking it. He had been thinking about how you willingly, for twenty-five years, suspend your id. How you become a model citizen for your children, the paragon they should emulate, a walking, talking saint, and after a while you lose who you are, you lose the attitude and the Corvette, you drop the bad hobbies and the bad friends, and you become a Little Green Man cut-out of the suburban dad. It would have been okay. It would have been a fair trade-off, except you discover that they haven't been buying it anyway. The children. They were doing whatever the hell they wanted, terrifying their poor mother until she could not sleep. So where did that get you? *Where?*

His father's secrets turned Chuck into a co-conspirator. And he wondered, more often than he cared to, what his mother knew. He wondered how much was apocryphal, how much was true. "Your uncle Rupert was married four times, once to a circus performer," and then one night, outside in the garage, a night imprinted in Chuck's brain: "Your mother had a friend years ago when I was away, a *friend*—" And which came first: his mother assigning his unremarkable brother the role of favourite or him being a co-conspirator in his parents' own Cold War? Because here is the thing about secrets, Chuck believed: people know there is something there; they just don't know *precisely* what it is. But they *know* there is something.

By the fifth day, Chuck was feeling different—he felt subversive walking into a grocery store where people had shopped for years. Browsing in the hunting-licence store that also sold birthday cards, ornaments, and rubber boots. Eating in a chain restaurant where no one knew him. Wearing a camo hoodie and a ball cap. He thought he was blending in when he wasn't.

Chuck admired a '73 Buick Riviera—boat-tailed and cream-coloured. He saw a man driving a scooter decorated with two black pirate flags, a mesh lawn chair strapped to the side with a bungee cord. The faux pirate didn't fool him. These were not frivolous people down here, Chuck had decided. After the *Miss Ally* sank two hundred kilometres from Halifax and the Coast Guard called off the search, word reached local divers, and they steamed for more than twenty hours in a flotilla of grief, and they said, "fuck this" and they strapped on their gear and they went down when it was too dangerous to go down, and they gave the families all they could ask for: closure. Chuck killed the tequila traveller he had poured in a Tims cup.

The cruellest betrayal a secret-keeper can experience is discovering that you aren't the only one, that something you struggled to protect had been shared with others. You are no longer special. And sometimes you find out by chance; sometimes you test the waters. Chuck needed to know. After his father was buried, his mother asked Chuck and Tony to sort through his things, to share what they wanted and give away the rest. And so the brothers went into his closet and his drawers and they bundled up his clothes. Hidden under socks, they uncovered a leather photo album and when they opened it, it contained nothing more sinister than photos of them. They found a lockable box with nine 7.62 Soviet cartridges, a photo of their mother in a flowered dress looking as happy as she had ever been. A set of brass knuckles. Smelling salts. Chuck found a kitschy ornament of a wooden lobster trap and he held it up for Tony, who looked nothing like him *or* his other siblings.

"Do you think he got this in Shag Harbour?" And Tony, the favourite, drew a blank.

*

Strange people show up down here from time to time. One day, two young men arrived and spent hours walking up and down the main street under an unusually bright sun, past the grocery store and the car wash. They wore black T-shirts with green fluorescent writing *JESUS JESUS JESUS*. Beaming otherworldly smiles, they handed out miniature comic books that asked, "Are you a good person?" After two days, they left.

On Cape Sable Island, there is a sandy beach where dozens of tiny birds put on the most delightful show, running in and out with the tide. Chuck stood there and watched them for an hour, his mind shifting to a quiet blue space. He thought about all of the years he had been terrified of being caught with secrets, and how that fear, that burden, was permanently printed on the liner notes of his life.

And was it any surprise that his two sons were hellions, as wild as their grandfather? They drove Hardtail Harleys. Nathan was a roadie for a Norwegian thrasher band and was married to a neopagan woman named Rikke whom Chuck had yet to meet. Max was an undercover cop who had infiltrated a Montréal drug ring backed by the Hells Angels and the Mob. Was it any surprise with those genes?

Chuck watched the birds and after a while he became so entranced, so hypnotized, that he told himself that it would work—that he and his wife could move here and nobody would notice. They could slip in on the fog. They could have things just the way they wanted them.

Chuck got in the van and he drove past a restaurant named after the *Miss Ally*'s lost captain, younger than both his boys. The air was as clear as his thoughts. Chuck drove until he spotted a red Charger in a Shag Harbour driveway, and he knocked on the door. His father had described it so vividly, so often... "Why, hello. No, not a problem." And then Chuck went inside and told Laurie Wickens everything he knew.

Skunk Boy

How do you double the value of a Pontiac Aztek?
Fill it up with gas.

Caspar's father, Stan, was uncommonly fond of costumes and would find any excuse to don one. Stan, who had a voice as weak as dollar-store cologne, performed in church operettas, allowing him to dress up as a Roman sentry, a pirate, and Iolanthe's half-fairy son.

Stan volunteered with the Boy Scouts, not because he enjoyed tying square knots around a campfire but because it allowed him to wear a neckerchief. He joined a group of historical re-enactors and ordered a faux coonskin cap. He moonlighted as a commissionaire. Stan purchased a polka-dot Tour de France cap and he drove his eighteen-speed Huffy through town precisely once, running into a pink hydrangea in full and glorious bloom.

Nothing made Stan feel more potent, more especial, than putting on a costume *ex cathedra*, and if the costume could be construed as a mark of authority or power, no matter how trifling, so much the better.

All of this *somehow* contributed to Caspar's peculiar personality, which was, from childhood, as pronounced as his terrible awful limp. Caspar was, from the time he was old enough to register as an individual, an outlier: the square peg in the round hole, as singularly odd as Stan's collection of hats. He had noisy black hair dissected by a thick white stripe and when he was a child, people called him Skunk Boy.

That's who Caspar is.

It's not just his current condition—the one I am here to assist with—that makes people uncomfortable, that makes them slide across the street to avoid him, as though he was a do-gooder in a Panama hat collecting money for cat neutering. Caspar has always been hard to take.

That's my humble point.

On this day, the day after Easter Sunday—after the baked ham supper and the chocolate mini eggs—there was no suggestion that there would be an incident at the PEI nursing home where Caspar works. No grim foreshadowing. No bird striking a plate-glass window.

Like most dilemmas in this life, it came upon us without warning. And before we knew it, Caspar and I were hovering like ruby-throated hummingbirds outside a radio booth, trying to catch the full attention of a retired lawyer named Eric T. Hamish, an uninvited guest of the Seaview Manor Broadcasting Club. Eric, who days earlier had been lying in his room, as motionless as the Saviour on Good Friday. Eric who had risen from the dead with a vengeance.

ON AIR says the red light above the glass door. Caspar and I can both see inside the booth. We can both see Roy, the radio show's host, in his chair, with Eric across from him in a chair that is supposed to be empty. Roy is wearing a golf shirt, Eric a long-sleeved dress shirt one might wear to a wedding.

Caspar waits until Roy puts a new song on before he takes it upon himself to address Eric, ensuring that Roy's microphone is off.

"Eric," he shouts loud enough to be heard in the great state of Mississippi. "What's the difference between a dead skunk in the road and a dead lawyer?"

Pause.

"There are skid marks in front of the skunk."

Caspar was summoned to negotiate with Eric, eighty-six, *not* to tell lawyer jokes. He was summoned because normally Caspar knows how to deal with Eric, who is in the early stages of dementia and can become aggressive if he feels the slight bit threatened.

"That's a two, Caspar," Eric shouts back. "That's a two."

Roy, who is accustomed to the habits of both Eric and Caspar, carries on as though nothing is amiss.

Caspar has anxiety, but he also suffers from an unfortunate condition named *Witzelsucht*, which translates from German to "joke addiction." Doctors believe that *Witzelsucht* is caused by brain damage to the right frontal cortex that, in turn, was caused by an aneurysm. In any event, it makes the sufferer insufferable. Caspar tells terrible jokes from the moment he gets up in the morning until he climbs into bed at night. He is the car alarm that will not cease, the co-worker who keeps talking American politics as though he is the only one who truly understands it.

Caspar tells his own jokes. How do you double the value of a Pontiac Aztec?

He tells old ones as stale as a lifetime of grievances. A rabbi a priest and a minister walk into the bar —

Unlike real comedians who feed off their audiences, who adjust their sails with the prevailing mood, Caspar is oblivious to the shifts — the compulsion is in the telling of the joke and not the validation he receives, for usually there is none.

"Why don't cows ever have any money?

"Because the farmers milk them dry!"

Caspar tells another bad joke while he is supposed to be managing Eric, who this time chooses to ignore him. A gerontologist determined that Eric has *frontotemporal dementia*, which can make him forget words and seem uncaring to others. It comes and goes. There are days when he cannot remember anything and there are days when he can freely quote Balzac and F. Lee Bailey.

A retirement home is a bit like high school. Most people don't want to be there, but some make the best of it, joining committees and little clubs, racking up credits for their next life, while others resist. They skulk, they disengage, their misery palpable. They hold a radio show host named Roy hostage.

Eric, much like Caspar, is hard to like. Eric was never a handsome man, but in old age his body's infrastructure has collapsed, and when he sits at a table, his chin and stomach almost touch. Eric doesn't boast about being the smartest person in the room but he cannot hide it and that makes the others avoid him.

Eric did throw a compliment my way once, telling Caspar, "That's not a bad-looking dog you have. How does he stand you?"

"He's paid to like me," Caspar replied, and then he laughed at his own stale joke.

My name is Beau and I am a comfort dog and I was assigned to Caspar two years ago after I received my training in a Florida prison. I could have coyly strung you along for several pages and then sprung it on you in a literary gotcha—*What? He's a dog!!*—but what's the good of that?

Caspar tries again: "Hey, Eric, why are they using lawyers instead of rats in lab experiments?"

Pause.

"There are some things rats won't do."

When Caspar tells a joke, he tells it defiantly, with an aggressive sniff at the end. And then his eyes go a little cuckoo.

Except for his skunk hair, his terrible limp, and the cuckoo eyes, there is nothing exceptional about Caspar's appearance. No clues to his rare disorder. He could be your oddball parking attendant or the postman who wears shorts all winter, a podgy forty-five-year-old ding-dong who smiles too much.

"Shut up, Caspar," shouts Eric.

I rarely see Eric with anyone at the Manor; he seems as alone as a beggar. Compared to most of the residents, Eric is an educated man. A man of means. I truly do not know why he is in Seaview and not one of the posh facilities with a real ocean view and gourmet food. I reckon that his children are getting him back for something—for being smarter than they are, for knowing it. At Seaview, everyone has their own room, three meals a day, and for the more mobile, a weekly bus trip to Wal-Mart, but the building is, I am the first to admit, frill free, with a *Khrushchyovka* feel.

On air, Roy remains as cheerful as a meadow of golden wildflowers, unbothered by the fact that Eric burst into the studio twenty minutes ago and refuses to leave. That is Roy's nature. When he moved into Seaview last year, he carried a large old notebook stuffed with newspaper clippings secured with a red elastic band. He carried it like a Bible.

Roy tells listeners: "And that was Glenn Miller with 'Blueberry Hill.' The request came from Margaret, who is recovering from bypass surgery."

Roy was happy to join the broadcasting club after he moved in. His show is pumped into common rooms and transmitted across PEI by a cable TV station. Around two thousand listeners tune in, mostly seniors—folks who own black-and-white photos with the year stamped in the margin, love letters written by hand. Memories of kerosene lamps and livery stables. Wartime telegrams that would break your heart.

Roy, it seems, has now decided to make the best of Eric's uninvited presence.

"We have a surprise visitor: Eric from the fourth floor. Eric, who is a lawyer, has offered to give us free legal advice," Roy tells listeners.

"My pleasure, Roy," says Eric, who has a microphone on his side of the table, one usually reserved for invited guests.

"Now, Eric. What can you tell us about wills?"

"Leave nothing to the little bastards, who will just buy cedar cottages and trips to Cambodia. Leave it all to an animal — an animal —" He sputters to a stop, unable to remember the word.

"Thank you for that useful advice, Eric," says Roy. "Wills are very important."

Roy, who worked as a barber for forty years, is everyone's favourite. Lean and noiseless in white sneakers, he moves as though he is on wheels, a twinkle in his eye. All of the ladies love him; Roy is as welcome as a cup of sweet tea, as comforting as the rolling green field behind the home that the old men sit and stare at for hours.

In a place like this, there is an odd rhythm: some people move along just fine, but time has to wait for others, the ones who need walkers or wheelchairs, the ones rooted to one place by melancholy or the feeling they have done enough. They have earned their stillness, they have earned their goodbyes.

"Do you have any other legal advice?" Roy asks.

"Lie!" says Eric without a second's hesitation. "The legal system is based firmly on lying; we professionals call it 'zealous advocacy,' so you must lie! 'Any fool can make a rule, and any fool will mind it.' That is Thoreau, by the way."

Eric doesn't sound like some of the others who say "haych" and "warsh," and utter phrases like "we lived handy the water"—the old farmers who wear soft plaid shirts and blue suspenders, their hands tattooed by the sun. He sounds like he has just come from lunch at the lieutenant-governor's.

Eric has left the chair, and he is looming, a rubbery, brainy hulk, over Roy.

Roy ends each and every show with Hank Snow's "I'm Moving On." On Roy's show, listeners call in with requests, sometimes the same song over and over again. When Mabel from Iona stopped calling to ask for Vera Lynn's "We'll Meet Again," people knew that her wish had come true.

Roy decides not to react to Eric's closeness and instead delivers another announcement. "Today is Myra Gallagher's ninety-eighth birthday, and her granddaughter is coming in from Souris."

Caspar for once says nothing. That is unusual. He is rarely quiet. When Caspar enters a room, any room, he brings with him an aura of discomfort—it makes people clench their jaws, it makes them sit at unnatural angles with one eye on the door.

Roy finishes playing a classic and says, "And that was the great Wilf Carter with 'You'll Get Used to It.'"

"And don't we all?" Eric is not supposed to be talking now.

Roy decides to roll with it. What else can he do?

"Yes, we do, Eric, yes we do. You said during that last song that you had something you wanted to share."

Eric leans down so that he is speaking directly into Roy's microphone.

"The Stuart Wishmore murder case, the alderman charged with killing his wife in 1972. I defended Wishmore, who was acquitted of all, ah, all—Anywho, he was guilty as hell. He shot her with a hunting rifle because she was having an affair with a judge, and the judge was... he was... Anywho, I will get back to you on that one."

"Thank you, Eric," says Roy. "Very interesting."

And then Caspar shouts through the door: "Everybody knew he was guilty. But you're going to have to leave now. Roy needs to get to his exercise class—"

"Shut up, Caspar," Eric yells back. "You're not talking to a fool."

Last week, Caspar and I went to a funeral home with Stan, who wore a black Dracula cape. We went to pay our respects to a cousin named Jack McCready, who was laid out splendidly on white satin. Caspar stood over the mahogany casket and blurted, "Jack in the Box. Does he come with a prize—a decoder ring?" And no one laughed.

Some say I drew the short straw when I got Caspar, but I like to think that Caspar got me because I am—and please don't interpret this is as vanity—likeable, while Caspar is not. I come from the South where manners grow on peach trees, where people call you "honey" and "pumpkin." In Virginia, they have Civil War ghosts and runaway-truck ramps. Billboards that ask: *Where are you going: Heaven or Hell?* One day, I was riding down the interstate behind a car, and its back window had been covered with letters made from black tape:

RIP
Uncle James

and when I passed, I saw a teenage girl driving with the window open, tears streaming down her face. It's like that in the South, y'all; it's different.

Roy tells listeners that he will be playing three of their favourite wartime songs uninterrupted. He makes that sound as inviting as a Sunday afternoon drive in the countryside. Roy comes out of the booth to take a break from Eric—he finally seems tired of the whole thing. Caspar makes a joke about adult diapers—

"What kind of underwear does Donald Trump wear?"

Pause.

"Depends."

Roy goes back in.

When Caspar was in his twenties, he drove a moped

with the licence plate *I ♥ the Single Life*. He collected Happy Meal toys at yard sales. Caspar's current affliction serves to exaggerate his already odd personality. It is a type of piling on if you will, which makes it hard for people to separate the old him from the new him; it makes it hard for them to understand.

•

Two women residents shuffle over to see what is up, and I move closer to Caspar's feet, rubbing his leg to calm him. We are still outside the booth, Roy and Eric still inside.

They are sisters, so they always have the benefit of a sidekick. Their hair is dyed the same shade of taupe. Miss Bessie is bossy and loud, while Miss Edna is meek and muffled. I know that Miss Bessie doesn't care for Caspar; one day I heard her tell him to, "Put a cork in it, Skunk."

I sniff the air. Anxiety smells like bleach, and the scent tells me when Caspar needs me, when someone is making him panic, like the obdurate passport clerk who threatened to call Security because he made a joke, or Stan who keeps visiting Caspar after work when all Caspar wants to do is decompress, to let his nerves settle down like a tired old sofa set out on a porch to rest. To play his online game EverWing.

Caspar says hello to the elderly sisters, and then asks, because he cannot help himself, "Were trees invented when you were born, Bessie?"

"Trees!" Bessie looks like she could bite his head off. Her sister half smiles.

Miss Bessie lords over her sister, believing she is better

at everything. But when they are apart, Miss Edna strikes up conversations with the other residents, complimenting them on their hair or their grandchildren. Edna knows how to make people like her; this is the little trick she has on Bessie.

The sisters are quickly bored with Eric's situation—he is not talking anymore, he is back in a chair—and they start to argue with each other the way they always do.

"Did you read that more women get Alzheimer's?" demands Miss Bessie of her acquiescent sister.

"Yes."

"No, you didn't. You never read anything."

"Yes, I did."

"Well, seventy-two per cent are women."

"That's because women live longer."

"No!" Miss Bessie shouts, outraged. "Because they don't keep their brains active."

"Marjorie Arsenault taught nursing—"

"Marjorie never used her brain. She never used her brain like I do."

"I guess you are right."

"Of course I am right."

Miss Edna just shrugs.

Miss Edna's room is papered with pictures of her late husband, who was handsome in his youth: he wore a tan fedora in the fifties and a sailor suit during the war. Miss Edna kisses the photos each night, and I know that she considers her life without him a test, a period that she must get through with as much cheer as it takes, until they are, which is all she dreams of, reunited.

Miss Bessie has no pictures of her husband on display, and the only visitor she gets is a ragamuffin grandson named AJ, who wears an unofficial Slipknot sweatshirt with a menacing skull. AJ favours Mecca jeans with embroidered pockets. "He's so smart," Miss Bessie tells her sister. "If only he would apply himself. He is so smart."

The two sisters are still standing near us bickering, so Caspar takes advantage of their proximity. He asks Miss Bessie: "Did you know I have a half-sister?"

"No." Miss Bessie goes for it despite herself. "Different fathers?"

I nudge Caspar's good leg, pretending that I need to go outside, but it is futile. I can no more stop him than I can stop a house cat from killing a yellow songbird.

"No," Caspar replies, "shark."

Miss Bessie gives me the same look she always gives me, the one that asks, "Are you still here?" And then she scowls at Caspar and leaves.

•

"Why do they charge you fifty dollars to leave PEI?

"They don't know you would pay one hundred."

Caspar tells that joke to a man passing by in a wheelchair. When the man does not respond Caspar tries again: "My cousin Larry is so ugly he has to sneak up on his mirror." This time the man just shakes his head, and I can hear him thinking, *What kind of foolishness is this?*

Sometimes, I think it's a mean trick that Caspar was born on PEI, a mannerly, peaceful island, an island that has, to the best of my knowledge, never produced a single successful stand-up comic. He might have been born in that *other* island province—the mad, untamed one brimming with cheeky comic genius. He might have seemed less odd there.

Caspar and I live above a boutique ice cream store that caters to mannerly, peaceful tourists. Outside our window is a banner of a strawberry ice cream cone that flaps like laundered sheets on a breezy day. I cannot look across the street—at the yoga studio and the fair-trade coffee shop—without seeing that ice cream flapping.

We moved downtown, away from Stan's suburban bungalow, to be edgy, but the ice cream almost ruins it. There is so much symbolism, so many clichés: broken-hearted women eating it from the tub, children being subdued with it, young lovers licking it. Caspar gave me ice cream one day, but I don't care for it. No matter how human he thinks I am, the truth remains: I am a dog, a six-year-old golden retriever who weighs seventy pounds and likes to drive with my head out the car window.

People who have *Witzelsucht* are supposed to be unaware of their impact on others. But here is what others do not see: they do not see Caspar alone at night, in that private moment, that terrifying time, when he realizes that the whole world hates him.

I am here to assure him that I don't, that I see past the bad jokes and the racing heart, and I tell him, and please excuse my language, *Damn them if they can't take a joke.*

And then it happens. Eric just walks out of the booth without even a goodbye to Roy. It is over. Eric is subdued now. The retired lawyer mutters something about a judge nicknamed Humpy who has a cocaine problem. Caspar makes another joke even though I know he is so anxious that he could explode.

"Why did God create snakes before lawyers?"

"I dunno, Caspar."

"He needed practice."

"Enough of the lawyer jokes, Caspar."

We slowly make our way back to Eric's room as though we are mourners who have just left a funeral. Eric is leading, I am last. In the hallway is a poster for a sock hop that will feature hamburgers and cake. *Dress in your 50's or 60's outfit and you could win a prize! Prizes for Spot Dances too!*

We shuffle past a long window that catches our reflection, and Eric sighs, "Sometimes I look in a mirror and I see Gregory Peck. How is that for a joke?"

Caspar and I take a short calming-down break in the employee lounge. Caspar drinks a bottle of orange juice, and I lick my paw. The panic is subsiding.

The doctors say that Caspar could have suffered the aneurysm at any time, the anxiety was pre-existing, and that they treated with drugs that made him worse. At one point, he could not sleep; at another, he was suicidal. One day, he had a panic attack on the thirteen-kilometre-long

Confederation Bridge. He stopped his car and he stayed there—suspended between two provinces—until they sent someone out.

There are bad days for Caspar. And there are worse ones like the days when he recalls, in dreadful detail, the sunny summer day that Stan, distracted, drove his 1976 Oldsmobile Custom Cruiser into a tractor, killing his wife and fracturing Caspar's young skull. Stan who just wants Caspar to tell him it wasn't his fault, when it was.

Some folks will help you, no strings attached. And then there are the others, the ones who demand something valuable back: your dignity, your hope, your belief that life will someday right itself. They insist that you strip naked and declare—without the slightest reservation—that you are mentally ill, a drug addict, a prostitute, or an abused child, when that is not *you.* That is just *a part* of you, a part you hope to someday leave behind.

I think that Caspar's joke-telling affliction is his final test. He is the bridge that engineering students build of wood and glue, that is then tested to see if it will support five-thousand pounds of weight. Those tests are done to save us from collapsing bridges in real life, and I cannot tell you why Caspar is being tested, why the weight is being heaped upon him. I do not know what lives will be saved by this.

*

Our break is over and we are walking down the hall. Caspar nods at a woman who is cradling a doll, a round-faced baby in a white nightgown that she holds as lovingly as she once held her real round-faced babies. The doll has a white bow on its head. The woman kisses it. People here are no different than people anywhere else; it is just that their strengths and weaknesses are exposed. There is no place to hide them. Kindness, arrogance, meanness, sadness.

It is twenty minutes since Roy played his sign-off song, "I'm Moving On." Caspar sees a *Do Not Disturb* sign on Roy's closed door, and instead of knocking, Caspar goes right in. That's what Caspar does, and everyone knows it.

"Hello, Roy," says Caspar.

Roy is sitting on the side of his bed and he looks different. It's the weekends that are hard here; it's the weekends when folks get lonely. Roy is still wearing his sneakers but he looks as though he has succumbed to the sadness that old people succumb to: the cumulative loss that cannot be shaken off with a brisk walk or an evening at bowling. His sadness sounds like ice cracking on a lake at night.

Next to Roy's bed are his dentures and a photo of a young woman with squinty eyes and a giant smile. She is wearing a red *Canada* jacket and she looks as robust as anyone I have ever seen. Caspar, after a glance at the photo, volunteers, "I hear that your granddaughter was on the national ski team."

And then—just like you were watching a movie on the Space Channel—something peculiar happens. All of the slack muscles in Roy's face connect, and there he is, on the coldest day of the year, standing at the bottom of a ski hill in Schladming, Austria, with every dream he had ever had racing through turns at one hundred kilometres an hour with a number on her back. Praying harder than you have ever prayed for anything in your life.

"Ten years. Plus the ten she put in before that."

"Must have been intense."

"You could say that," Roy laughs. "The money her parents poured into that. She had guts, Caspar, she had guts."

And so, I hold my breath, waiting for Caspar to make a bad joke. And then I realize that Roy will not hear him. Roy has gone to *that* place, the sunny one that reminds him that his time on Earth was not wasted, that place that puts the twinkle in his eye and the lightness in his step, the same place that Miss Edna goes to with her handsome sailor. He is, for a blessed time, happy.

Days before this whole incident with Eric, Miss Bessie's grandson came to visit in his Slipknot sweatshirt. When he stepped off the elevator, he cocked his chin as though he was there to solve a weighty problem: the internet or the lunch menu. He isn't fooling anyone, I dare say, except Miss Bessie. Every time AJ visits, he tells his grandmother a sob story. Every time, she gives him money. One day, AJ told her that his pug needed emergency surgery, when he doesn't have a pug.

AJ and Miss Bessie always meet in the common room, which is big enough for a Christmas concert by schoolchildren or for Wednesday night bingo. One day, Miss Edna joined them and she whispered to AJ, "The nurses tell me that I look young for my age," and Miss Bessie heard her and snapped, "Oh Edna, they are pulling your leg."

On this day, it was just Miss Bessie and her shifty grandson. After five minutes, AJ announced that he was going to the washroom. Caspar and I followed him down the hall, suspicious. We saw him duck into Miss Bessie's room, where we caught him red-handed.

"Hey, Big Pussy Bonpensiero," ordered Caspar, "put down the purse."

Caspar isn't a strong man, but he tried to look fearless, he tried to look like Tony Soprano, and AJ called his bluff. He raised his arms up like a football blocker and he hammered Caspar straight to the floor. *Bang!!* his striped head crashing with the most awful sound. I feared for a moment that AJ had knocked him out cold.

And then—just like I was watching a bright red ball roll across the floor in my direction—I saw my chance, the one I had been waiting for since I first laid eyes on AJ's sorry ass. I sunk my teeth through his Mecca jeans and I bit him.

Here is what you need to know about Caspar before you cast him into life's human junk pile, along with the liars, the betrayers, and the trifling ne'er-do-wells who never experience the ephemeral joy of good intentions. Caspar didn't tell Miss Bessie that her ragamuffin grandson was a no-good thief who had assaulted him. He didn't tell anyone, even though Miss Bessie calls him behind his back, "Pepé Le Pew," the skunk who was always, in his own brash way, seeking love.

And that is my humble point.

Stan is visiting Caspar at our apartment and the air is unsettled. On edge. It is always like that when Stan is around—he is so wound up that you feel like you are caught in a game of dodge ball. Sometimes even I feel uneasy and *I* spent three months in a federal penitentiary. Stan is wearing a Shriners' suit with a purple fez and a look of mad desperation. The conical hat is perched on his head like he is an Ottoman ruler. I can tell that Caspar would like to tell Stan about his negotiations with Eric, he would like to tell him that he had an EverWing high score of 3800, but his father is so excited by his new costume that he cannot listen; he is so excited that he could, at that moment, forget who he really is.

Is That All You Got?

My grandfather was a prizefighter. Not a dilettante at a sports club with towel service and Zumba classes, but a guy who earned a living with his fists. Back in the days of six-ounce gloves, epic ten-rounders, and a cut man who could give you a second chance at glory.

"There's two kinds of fighters," according to Pops. "There's the poor bastards who go in the ring and they're fightin' for someone else: their wife, their old man—they want it so bad that it hurts to watch them. And then there's guys like me: I fought because I liked it; I liked every goddamn round."

Pops liked punching people in the face; he liked figuring out their weakness—he drops his right, he can't infight worth shit—he liked taking a left hook to the ribs and standing there like a mad Irish warrior: Is that all you got, you no-good dirty bastard?

He's ninety-six now with a smashed nose and dented knuckles. A flat cap that doesn't cover his elephant ears. The record book says that Pops aka Dew Drop Mahoney had 130 pro fights all over Canada and the US and that he moved through four weight classes like it was his job. Fifty-two knockouts, thirty TKOs. He was knocked out twice, and other times he got back up when a smarter man, a softer man, might not have.

A few years back, a salesman from Ontario came to Pops's house and said he might be his son.

"Go fuck yourself," Pops barked and then slammed the door.

"Well, that wasn't very nice," my grandmother sighed.

"Do I look like a goddamn babysitter?"

You can't make people care about you. They are going to be whoever they are going to be. And that is a mixture of genes and fate and life deciding that you should never get your hopes up. People can be savage. Some of that I learned from Pops, some of that the hard way.

Pops grew up blocks from where I am standing in downtown Charlottetown in a drafty house with an empty coal bin and an emptier cupboard. A lot has changed since Pops left at sixteen to fight a war—the neighbourhood is gentrified now, with five-star inns and yachts in the harbour. People expected Pops to mellow, to become gentrified himself, but he didn't. Some people are born rich, some smart. Pops was born tough. That's what he had, and, in hindsight, it seems unfair that people expected him to change, when that's all he had.

I was born a twin, and that's a blessing and a curse, just like Pops's toughness. I think Pops calls me "Girlie" because he can't tell us apart. Courtney or Chloe? If you knew us, you'd know that we are nothing alike—I was born two minutes earlier and I'm exactly one centimetre taller.

We do totally different work, me and my twin. I am a freelance designer who works from home on my MacBook.

I design photo books, memoirs. I just finished a graphic novel about a boy who runs away from home with a roan Newfoundland pony named Skipper Jack. I really like my cover. Courtney studied hotel/motel management and works at the front desk of a hotel. She likes it; she says there is always room for promotion in the hotel business.

*

It's 9:55 a.m. I have an appointment for an apartment viewing for 10 a.m.

Two strangers are standing with me in front of a two-storey wooden house. The man reminds me of my cousin Andrew who once trapped a bat in Pops's barn and brought it to school where it escaped. So I name him Andrew after my cousin, who has awkward ears and rubbery limbs.

Ten minutes pass. It's 10:05.

Everything moves slowly on Prince Edward Island: cars, tractors, the Japanese tourists in floppy hats who meander through the streets in summer bewitched by a red-haired myth. Life cannot be rushed. The CBC did a story about a woman who kept a snowball in her freezer for fifteen years, another about a man who suspected someone had secretly cut his horse's hair. That's the Island for you. Dramatic.

"What time did she give you?" Andrew asks the woman standing with us, who is wearing a charm bracelet.

"Quarter to ten."

"Me, too." He tries to sound indignant. "She didn't tell me there would be others."

I stand on the sidewalk, shuffling from side to side. I have a humming in my ears, and it sounds like a cheap motel fridge that keeps you up all night; it sounds like someone's far-away phone set on vibrate, snaking its way across a table and onto the floor; it sounds like something that you checked every corner of the house for and could not find. And then the sky turns a cool shade of pink.

Other people's grandparents are dead or they go to the Kiwanis; they take bus trips to Maine. They collect Hummels. When someone asks me if I am related to Pops, I never know what to say; I never know if he worked with them or if he punched them in the face. As soon as they say Dew Drop, his ring name, I get nervous. Grandma, she's more normal.

One Christmas Pops told me, "I like you best when you're smiling, Girlie." It was his way of telling me not to take life so seriously: my parents' spectacular divorce, the fact that my identical twin suffers from narcissistic personality disorder. Stuff like that. *Life is cruel and capricious,* I wanted to tell him, *and we can be defined by one bad decision at an age when we are in no condition to make decisions.* I wanted to tell him, but I didn't.

Last night, I took an online test that tells you if you are an empath. I scored 21 out of 22. The only box I didn't tick was "has a low tolerance for pain." I know those tests are lame. I am the first to roll my eyes when the thickest people I know take the Test Your Vocabulary quiz and then proudly—without the slightest trace of self-awareness—boast, "I am a vocabulary genius!" No, you are not. Everyone on Earth knows the difference between "antidote" and "anecdote"; they know that "chimley" is not a real word. They know that the answer to this Test Your Vocabulary Test is not A:

I would have come earlier if I _________.
had knowed
have known
had known

But who am I to talk? If I were a true empath, someone who absorbs the feelings of others, someone who anticipates their pain and joy, I would have known that my twin worries more about Mike from *Better Call Saul* than she does about me.

I hope they don't kill him.

Well, they do.

I went to Courtney's apartment to give her a surprise gift. When I showed up, DAVIDsTea in hand, I apologized, admitting I had been messed up since that thing with my apartment. The reason I am moving. I feel guilty over everything, you see. Some days, I feel guilty for existing—a meta-emotional mess.

Apartment thing? She squinted, so that she could see all of me.

And she didn't know. She didn't know anything at all about my life.

I can't even.

*

It is 10:15 a.m.

A white Vibe pulls up. It is a woman, and we all hope she is the person showing the apartment, but she isn't. This woman is wearing Hush Puppies and carrying a TOPS tote bag. She seems bereft, like one of those women who goes on a TV makeover show and has her long platinum hair chopped off into a mud-brown bob, and the host gushes, "This is our best makeover yet," and she is holding back tears. Gutted. Because her new hair looks like garbage.

Andrew looks at his watch again. "I been up since crow piss."

He doesn't acknowledge me.

I have been invisible for weeks now. I used to go into stores and feel people staring at me, measuring me. Comparing me. I would feel obliged to make small talk and sometimes I would say the right thing, but more often than not, I would leave feeling awful. When I looked in mirrors, my ears were red and my head was shaped like a deformed potato.

And then, because I willed it to happen, it happened: I disappeared. Mostly. There are moments, like now, when people can see me, but I am a ghost image that has appeared on an old negative by mistake, laid over another image. Smudged. I am *kind of/sort of there*, but I am not.

*

Pops and Grandma moved outside town after he retired from the city maintenance department. It is nice there with foxes and horses that harvest Irish moss. He has a workshop. Shelves of WD-40, glue, and jars of screws. Two coconut ornaments, one a monkey with wire glasses. Sometimes, we go to see them, me and my dad, who drives a Ducati. Sometimes, Courtney goes instead. It doesn't matter; Pops calls both of us "Girlie."

Sometimes, I see my grandparents' neighbours Yolanda and Edgar. He works in a lobster pound and she is a teacher. After years of marriage, they decided to have a child, and then, to their surprise they had twins, and both of the boys, two lovely boys, had Down's syndrome. And the narrative changed, at least for Edgar. There would be no early-morning hockey, no NHL tryouts. But there *would* be love—Edgar could guarantee that. It would have to be sheltered. It could not survive amid the loud boasts of our Darwinian world. Instead it would be quiet and kind, and the family would create their own world, and they could become experts on wildflowers. That's what they would do.

Edgar and the boys would spend hours outdoors, on cliffs and in forests, in fields and on sand dunes. Finding flowers: twinflower (*Linnaea borealis*). And photographing them: downy yellow violet (*Viola pubescens*). And cataloguing them: blue-flag iris (*Iris versicolor*). And sharing their knowledge. They decided that's what they would do; and they did.

It became normal to see Edgar, Moses, and Ben heading out with books and cameras. But by the time the boys reached eleven or twelve, they became less interested—they had their own friends, they liked more vigorous pursuits. So it became just Edgar.

And that's what Edgar does to this day. He chases wildflowers.

Life changes you in ways you could never predict. No one would have thought that Edgar would publish two books on wildflowers, and no one would have thought that Ben and Moses would go to the Special Olympics for track and field, but all of that happened.

*

There are five of us now waiting on the struggle bus.

Me. Andrew. The TOPS woman. The charm-bracelet woman and a tremendously fat man who is wearing shorts and support stockings for edema, with black elastic at the knees. He has trouble breathing; his enormous stomach seems to be crushing his airway.

"What time did she give you?"

"Ten twenty," the fat man wheezes. "I don't believe this."

"Me too," says Andrew. "This is crooked as a crowbar."

There is a text on my phone. *I can't even*, I think.

When I went to Courtney's apartment, her new friend was there: a Japanese girl. She was wearing a white blouse with a high collar and a cotton skirt. Ankle socks and black Mary Janes. She had an iPhone 5 in a white-and-pink teddy bear gel case. Courtney's new friend was staring at my twin's red hair as though it was the most amazing thing in the world, and they watched *Better Call Saul* without me.

It is 10:45 a.m. A waiting game.

The fat man is sitting on the curb, calling everyone "buddy." "I got the patience of a fence horse, buddy."

Andrew tells the charm-bracelet woman that he works in a steak house, and she tells him: "I worked at the hospital. I hurt my back, and they got rid of me."

The TOPS woman is ready to bounce, I can tell. The fat man makes her uneasy.

This apartment is a find. It is two bedrooms for only $700 a month. It is walking distance to the Cows ice cream store.

Nobody talks to me, not even Andrew.

Becoming invisible did not happen by itself; I started by making myself still; I let my body go numb; I held it until the urge to speak or be noticed passed. I worked on controlling my heart rate, my respiration rate, my blood pressure, and muscular movement. The best analogy I can give you is sand. I was like sand dumped on a city beach at the start of summer. Because I put up no resistance, I was slowly and gradually washed away.

A Kia pulls up. The driver looks like someone's dad, not mine, but someone's. It feels weird competing with a fifty-year-old man for an apartment, but here we are. The dad is wearing the caramel-coloured suit of a failed real estate salesman.

I check my texts. Courtney. *Well*, I think, *that is interesting.*

Last week, I took another online test: *What dog do you look like?* You upload your picture and it tells you. Someone uploaded their actual poodle and the test said it looked like an Airedale terrier. I uploaded my picture and it said I was a bull mastiff, and I uploaded my identical twin and it said she was a cockapoo. Life is nothing but a series of comparisons, isn't it? And one person always has to be better than the other.

"What time did she give you?"

"Ten thirty."

Three weeks ago, I went for a walk with my dad. My dad plays Jackson Browne albums and wears his hair in a zipper cut. He is mired in the seventies, which is before they figured out that divorce is not better for the kids; it's just better *for you* because it allows you to date inappropriate women, smoke weed on your deck, and buy a stand-up paddleboard that makes you think you are hip.

My dad had just watched a documentary about the Eagles on Netflix and he was telling me about it. My dad thinks people are more interested in his stories than they are. That's one of his biggest problems. That and the weed.

About a block from my basement apartment, two men were standing chest to chest on the sidewalk, and the older one was waving his finger in the face of the younger one, a jogger. The older man looked hotheaded. Thick and as volatile as a sausage. The jogger was one of those skinny men in his thirties, the passive-aggressive type, the kind of man who thinks jogging makes him more virtuous than the rest of us. I recognized him. One day I had seen him, while he was running, pound the hood of an old lady's car with his fist because he didn't like the way she had stopped at a crosswalk. *Bam bam bam*. Yelling.

This fight was over the dog. I concluded that the dog—a Jack Russell terrier—may have nipped the jogger, who may have retaliated with a kick. After that, the jogger could have continued running, but he had elected to backtrack and argue with the human sausage, and my father could have minded his own business, but he didn't.

He decided to be a hero.

And so the whole thing unfolded, with my father telling the men to settle down and "show some maturity," and the jogger telling him to "fuck off, asshole," and me trying to be invisible. And the jogger going nuts. "I told you: 'fuck off, asshole.'"

"I am glad I did that," my father later protested, which is how he justifies every stupid thing he has ever done in his life. Quitting his job at the post office to become an "art photographer," growing a soul patch, buying a pair of pricey white Oakleys he then had to wear for the next six years. Showing up uninvited at my mother's wedding to Pam.

And of course, the jogger lives across the street from me, and he is, as luck would have it, a very angry cop. Which is why I have to move.

He is watching me, waiting for an excuse to go off.

And some days he can see me.

Andrew looks at his watch. "I got work."

I want this apartment, so I am prepared to wait it out; I read a text.

There are some people you will never tell on because, despite how much they hurt you, you love them deep down in a place you can't control. And you can't tell on them anyway, because making them smaller would make you smaller, and you can't afford to get any smaller than this. What is there after invisible?

A motorcycle pulls up. "Is this her?" someone asks.

It is 11:00 a.m.

A woman emerges from the house next door. She resembles a French bulldog if French bulldogs wore leopard print slippers and a Shania Twain T-shirt. "You here for the apartment?"

Someone answers, "Yes."

"I don't know if I should be telling you, but there's a problem with the heat in that unit. The pipes freeze."

We nod thanks.

"And someone died in there—"

"Oh really?"

"Possibly murdered."

Maybe, I think.

Every town has its quota of sketchy people, even on PEI. In Charlottetown you used to see them near the statue of Sir John A. Macdonald sitting on a bench pondering the future of Canada, which PEI took its sweet time to join. Or panhandling outside the liquor store. One guy has long grey hair and he always wears shades, a pink fanny pack, and no shirt. They call him Snake Eyes.

The charm-bracelet woman says, "That's it, I'm leaving."

"Okay."

"The location is nice," offers the dad hopefully.

"Oh yes, I've lived here my whole life and the street is great, just great—" says the neighbour.

⁖

Pops's grandparents came here on a death ship from Ireland. Children died along the way and people were quarantined, and some of them died, too, and the town watched the parade of coffins from the dock, and maybe that stays in your blood. All of that. Pops thought no one should tell him how to live and maybe that's why boxing suited him. In the ring, you make your own decisions and you live by them. You win, you lose. You get your head punched off, your call. YOLO.

Pops's brother, Tom, was a boxer, too, but he was as sweet as Pops was hard. Tom had all the funny stories. He always identified the most marginalized person in the room and made them feel better. Sixty years after his last fight, Pops could be as mean as the night he went ten rounds in Madison Square Garden in a battle to the death with a man named Kid Caramel, who later did die in the ring. Sometimes, he'd even turn on his brother: "You no-good bastard; you never had a decent ten-rounder in your life." Pops calls everyone a "bastard." Sometimes it's an insult and sometimes it isn't. When Tom was dying, Pops stood by his hospital bed, hands folded. He turned his head so no one would see him cry, and it was as though he knew the sweetness was leaving, the sweetness that took the bite out of life.

Two more people come; two leave.

It is noon now.

"Well, that's it," says Andrew. "I'm history."

"Good luck."

"Good luck."

"Good luck."

Everyone bids him farewell. The TOPS woman follows.

I saw the angry cop last week and I think he saw me. I know he is going to get me; that's what bad cops do. I watched that season of *House* where the bad cop framed House because House disrespected him during an appointment. Just because we're in PEI doesn't mean it can't happen here.

I can't be that mad at my dad for forcing me to move—he never does anything on purpose. He is just bad at adulting. He took nude "art" photos of a girl who turned out to be my teacher's daughter. He crashed his Ducati with my twin on the back. ("The brain," Pops said, "of a Pekingese.") My father has a problem with cognitive dissonance; if something happens that he can't accept—like scientists linking weed to low productivity or my twin stealing my boyfriend—he gets stupid angry. "You two are exactly alike," he told me once. That's the worst thing he's ever said to me.

•

It is 2:00 p.m. Only me now.

The last person to leave was the fat man. I was afraid that he wasn't leaving because he couldn't get up, but finally he did, just as the sun ducked behind a cloud.

In the summer the Island explodes with ice cream booths, picnic tables with checkerboards painted on top, the Harbour Hippo. It's a carnival that folds its tent in the fall when farmers finish in the fields and the tourists leave. It's getting quiet now.

A text.

A car stops, and a woman sees my shadowy image. I am kind of/sort of there. I stand up tall and I think loud colours. Fuchsia. Tangerine. It works and she comes toward me. The woman is wan and ethereal like Queen Daenerys Targaryen from *Game of Thrones*. Her hair is in elaborate braids and she is wearing a floaty grey dress as though she has stepped out of a myth.

"I'm so sorry," she says. "My mother had a heart attack and I took her to the hospital. I've been there all day."

"No problem," I say. "Yep, no problem."

One afternoon, Courtney and I did our hair in Sansa's signature braid. We French braided the front sections of our hair backwards, then joined the two pieces and continued plaiting. After that, we pulled a few strands loose around our faces. We could have been in a medieval court;

we could have been in one of those *Vanity Fair* photo shoots where everyone is dressed in white and one person is lying across the front like a private school bitch.

"Can you come tomorrow and sign a lease?"

"Sure," I say, after another text from my twin. "Yep, sure."

•

Pops won a bunch of title fights but he never made any real money. He said he fought because he liked it, but maybe there was more to his story. What if you are the person your whole family is counting on—to lift them from their lot, to prove that life is not a rigged game of privilege and birthright and class, that you can, yes, you can, ascend—and then it all falls short? What if you are that person?

I'm not going to sugar-coat anything because Pops did tell that salesman to "go fuck yourself," and he could have been his son.

But I will tell you this: Pops went to every race that Moses and Ben were in, and he told them not to drink too much water before they ran because that was bullshit and everyone in the fight game knew it. Don't drink too much before a race. And while Edgar was chasing wildflowers, Pops made sure Ben's shoelaces were double-knotted. And when the boys lined up, they could have been Rocky Marciano and Jack Dempsey. Pops could have been a cut man with a bag full of tricks. And he smiled—he actually smiled—when the twins ran like hell. "Those boys are tough," he said, "they're as tough as Joey Jumpin' Giardello."

One day, I asked Pops if one of the twins was better than the other, and Pops gave me that look. The one where he stares at the ground, not me.

"They don't have time for that foolishness, Girlie."

I nodded and told him, "I don't either."

It's settled now. The apartment and everything. Courtney is going to help me make new curtains for the kitchen, different material this time. She is sorry that she didn't know that Dad made me move. What is wrong with him? she asks. I say no wonder Mom left him for Pam. Yeah. I tell her I'm sorry that I told her that they killed Mike. And she says that maybe she can move in with me again; it's always better that way, and I say, sure. She doesn't really like her new friend that much. The way she stares at her red hair and tries to touch it. Oh yeah, I say, that's weird.

What's It Like?

Twitter
The Globe and Mail
@globeandmail 34m
Are you on your third marriage? What's it like? Pros? Cons? Email our reporter Deidre Fairfield for a story: Xavierd@globem.com

To: Xavierd@globem.com
From: gregmac@yahoo.com
Yes, I am on my third. What's it like? Think back to when you were a teenager and imagine that you were the only kid in your neighbourhood forced to attend summer school because you had flunked algebra. It's that same feeling of dread and shame when you awake each morning. And the sun may be shining and your friends may be heading to Chesterman Beach in a van, but you are trudging to summer school, a failure. It's like *that.*

And you don't know why it happened. You tell yourself you were just lazy. People underestimate laziness. They mistakenly believe that underachieving children must be troubled, handicapped, or failed by their parents, when some are just lazy. You hope it is *that.*

But you fear it is something worse. You fear that you are so deficient that you may never be good at anything in life. Like summer school, a third marriage is your last chance—the one thing that stands between you and that dirt-road trailer with power lines running from someone else's house, a plastic rainwater collector, and an angry dog chained outside.

The pros: Christmas or Easter are never boring. When you have an extended and estranged family large enough to stage a full production of *Come from Away*—someone is bound to go off, and they always do. And it makes you question every decision you have ever made in your life, every road taken and not taken. And self-examination is a good thing, isn't it?

The cons: Think about it.

Robert

I would prefer that my real name not be used because—well, I am sure you know why.

Dear Robert,

Are you available for an interview about your worst Christmas? We could use your initials.

Cheers,

Deidre

*

From: MaeveandDonald@hotmail.com
Dear Miss Fairfield,

I struggled to find my path after many lost years during which I was distant from God. And then I was blessed when the elders instructed me to marry Donald, a good man whose wife died three months ago. I am grateful that I have the health to take care of Donald who is entering his ninetieth year, a blessing. Today was a wonderful day at the temple, where I did one endowment and Donald four. Next month, we are travelling to Utah, where Donald will do the sealing for his great-grandson. There I will meet the rest of his family before returning in time for my thirtieth birthday, which we will celebrate in our home.

Pros: The many blessings we share.

Cons: None.

Yours in God's image, Maeve

Dear Maeve,

Would you and your husband like to be in a photo?

Cheers,

Deidre

*

From: Mike@nili.ca
Dear Deidre,

I may be the only gay man in Canada with three legal marriages on the books. I think I was just so happy when we finally got our rights that I wanted in. And so I married a professor named Dennis—an expert in "the hierarchies of desirability via erotic capital in the value system of gay desire"—after two short months. What can I say about poor pedantic Dennis that has not been said before, that you cannot look up for yourself on RateMyProf, but I am not about to demonize Dennis. Not at all.

Dennis *was* a difficult person—and I say that with love—that person capable of making the most benign outing uncomfortable. I think of the time when we took his mother to dinner, and the waitress asked if we would like water, and Dennis replied with a resounding, "No!! I bring my own. I only drink well water." And then, for the duration of the meal, never took a sip.

After Dennis and I divorced—he kept the Gatineau farmhouse—I met Arthur. At this point you may cue the schmaltzy music, you may roll out every cliché about true love and happy ever after, because it was like that. It was. Arthur was perfect. A firefighter, he could fix things like pipes and roofs. He could cook. When you saw six-foot-two Arthur arriving at a party with a Tupperware container of lemon squares, your nervous system relaxed. You felt happy. Arthur would make the roses in your garden more glorious, a walk on the beach more exotic. Arthur would give you his last bottle of homemade Pinot Grigio or his best orbital sander, and make you feel like *you* had done *him* a favour. And then he died.

When you lose the love of your life... well, you lose the love of your life. After that, you may find a lesser love, you may find companionship, you may find a lovely man named Scott who will travel with you and who understands why you light a candle on Arthur's birthday and why you visit his mom at Christmas, why you collapse in a puddle of tears when a song comes on the radio. If you are lucky, you may…

Mike

Dear Mike,

Sorry for your loss. Is Scott okay with being in a story?

Cheers,

Deidre

From: hockeyfan10@hotmail.com

Dear Deidre,

Three times. Call me an optimist. When I got married at twenty-one, I built us a log house in Musquodoboit Harbour (NS). We were living the dream with two beautiful kids and a golden retriever named Rocket. If you ask me what went wrong, I will default to the oldest cliché in the books—*we were too young*—which means absolutely nothing. But I *will* tell you that my heart broke when that marriage ended. I loved that house as much as I loved Guy Lafleur.

On the rebound, I married Angie, the Kenny Linseman of spouses, master of the cheap dirty shot, which is all I will say about that. I was like a hitchhiker thumbing across the country, entering strange cars and strange towns with a sense of fearlessness that was, in hindsight, apathy. I didn't care enough about myself to be worried. I didn't care about my future. I was ready to take whatever life had aimed at me because, well, shag it.

Number three: I got it right this time. Gail is the sweetest woman you would ever meet. We live in Dartmouth, where we both grew up. Some goofs across the harbour call it Darkness and that's supposed to be a slag, but that's okay because Dartmouth has Joel Plaskett and Matt Mays who write songs about the town. Dartmouth has Sid the Kid and Nathan MacKinnon, while Halifax has the Rat. The Little Ball of Hate or whatever you want to call him, not that he cares. He's got a $49 million contract in Beantown where he is a hero, and that's $49 million more than you or I will ever see in our lives, so what the hell am I going on about anyway?

Pros: It's a journey.

Cons: I don't know what I am talking about half the time.

Greg

Dear Greg,

It sounds like you have found your perfect match. I may be in touch.

Best,

Deidre

From: AndreaJ@outlook.ca
Deidre,

What's it like? It's just life unfolding, just life, until vultures like you try to make a joke out of it, until you go trolling for out-of-context quotes and cringe-worthy details to feed on. *It's Jerry Springer time. Let's laugh at the freaks.*

I know how this works. I'm not stupid. Husband #2 was a crime reporter at *The Sun* until the cops found out he was working for the Mob.

You may know him. His business card says:

Jimmy Asshole
I'm two years behind on my child-support payments

Anyway, I know exactly what you are up to. But go ahead. Pretend that your life has been an Autobahn of Perfection. Mine hasn't. I am sure you will find some suckers to reply to you, to give you the anecdotes that make them look like fools. But not me. I am not going to help you with your "story," because you probably banged my worthless ex-husband anyway, and that was a wasted three minutes of your life, wasn't it?

Jimmy's ex

Dear Ex,

We at *The Globe* ensure that all of our stories are fair and balanced. I can assure you I have never been in a relationship with Jimmy. We were barely friends. If you change your mind about being in a story, please email. Your journey could help others.

All the best,

Deidre

⁂

From: gravedigger@ns.sympatico.ca

Dear Doris,

I'm on my marriage #3. I comes from a place so small that when you goes to Newport Confessions and Rants online you know who every anonymous poster is.

When someone writes: *Please someone tell me who is the sexy man with the bunny on a leash,* someone else right snappy tags Warren Bonang. And sure enough when you goes to his page, there he is with a rabbit. *Could someone tell me whose pig is on the loose?* gets six comments.

So when some greasy f&6k "confesses" that *I had sex with a married blond woman 30 crawling on 40 in a red car behind mcdonalds while her husband was at sea*, well—I pretty much knew the husband was me. That happened twice. Same greasy f&6k, same place. Only Wife #2 was in a white car.

There ain't no pros and there ain't no cons. Just keep on keeping on.

Billy Joe (aka Gravedigger)

Dear Billy Joe (Gravedigger),

You sound like you live in a colourful town. Thanks for your input.

All the best,

Deidre

*

From: Pandora@gmail.com
Dear Deidre,

Ever since I was a child, I wanted to get married to prove that I was lovable—I imagined the virginal dress, the hopeful cake, and the flower-draped tables of overjoyed guests there to celebrate Me. And now I know that I didn't prove anything. Marriage No. 1 to my high school crush Simon was a red-rose disaster. Marriage No. 2 to a co-worker named Al was a begonia bust. I'm now married to Ruby, and she is an amazing, wonderful gardenia of a woman, the best person I have ever known, and we both love Augustus Gloop who only eats chocolate and meat and we both fear dogs, but I realize that maybe I'm not cut out for this whole marriage thing. I am trying to find a way to leave without breaking her heart, and it's tough when hearts are involved. It's really tough.

Yours, Pandora

Dear Pandora,

Love your self-awareness.

"Try to be a rainbow in someone's cloud," Maya Angelou.

I may be in touch.

Deidre

From: BeverlyB@yahoo.com
Dear Deidre,

Office romances are like prison affairs—it's all about proximity and options. If I put you in an office with twelve deadly men, men you would never speak to in a wine bar, and I made you spend every day with them, by day 60 one would seem attractive. The guy with the feeble chin and Monty Python jokes. The fake Australian accent. The guy who bragged about being a slacker would eventually seem nice. Nicer than everyone else and quite possibly a kindred spirit. That's my story. Three office romances. Two divorces. Who knew?

Bev

Dear Bev,

Your candour is refreshing.

All the best,

Deidre

From: Thor@rotonmail.com
Dear beautiful Deidre,

I came across your tweet and your photo today, and I am hurt that you did not tell me you were a journalist. I am hurt that you did not give me your real name.

I know that you remember me. You took my card off the bar counter. *Bob's Flooring: High End Vinyl at Low Prices*, located on the ground floor of the Badger Mall in

Brampton. You said I had soft hands. You said you might never know when you might need a new floor. I am a gentleman so the rest is between us.

I am sure that the phony phone number you gave me was an honest mistake.

I'd like to see you again. For real.

Chad (Bob is not my real name).

Chad,

Never email me at work again or I will have you charged with stalking. I know that your name is not Bob. And it is not Chad either.

D

The Gates of Heaven

I am thinking about travelling to Denmark, where they are developing a pill to erase bad memories. Denmark, birthplace of Thumbelina, Hans Christian Andersen, and the tormented, tangled mind of Søren Kierkegaard, existentialist prince.

I am not certain who determines what memories are bad or how clean they can erase your mental hard drive. Is your mind like a computer, which means that nothing is truly gone, and that the IT investigators — the spooks with forensic software — can still recover your deleted porn and menacing emails?

But let's say that it works. Let's say I land in Copenhagen with a bag of gold and find the person with the magic potion. Maybe she is blithe and blond, a Danish princess. Or maybe he is a hunchbacked bachelor who looks like a toad.

I do not care about the philosophical debates that people are having: "How can one learn from one's mistakes if one cannot recall them?" or "The brain is wired to remember as a mechanism of survival." Those debates are immaterial to me, I would argue, given the last six years of my life. And to anyone who deigns to differ, I respectfully ask, "Who are you? The doorman at the Gates of Heaven?"

Life is not an Instagram photo with all the colours heightened and the background blown out. The Gates of Heaven are not manned by mortals, though it does help to have a reference letter, and some of those come in the form of obituaries. Obituaries are my primary field of study and form the research for my doctoral thesis, which I am endeavouring to complete, despite time lost, before I turn thirty. It is titled "Snapshots in Time: A Study of Obituaries in One Mid-sized Maritime Newspaper from 2000 to 2016."

Using established means, including a regexp for syntax highlighting, I am analyzing the obituaries of one Nova Scotia newspaper for sixteen years, noting sociological trends and/or changes. Most obituaries follow a template. Occasionally—often enough to merit a sub-category—there is a self-written entry, sometimes humorous, sometimes profound. There are fairy tales and hagiographies. Requests and wishful wishes.

> This qualitative exploratory study of obituaries was conducted in the grounded theory tradition. It is intended as a contribution to the sociological study of obituaries, a medium that conveys objective and subjective information about individuals and their lives, a medium devoid of verifiability.

I am maintaining a spreadsheet of individuals, who were, according to their obituaries, raised by non-parental family members, foster parents, orphanages, or other. To date — and I am nearing the end — I have documented one hundred and thirty, a number I cannot interpret, only report. My adviser is Doctor Kent Koopenhagen, a puffed-up penguin of a man who wears robes to lectures and talks at parties about the Cartesian mind until people's eyes glaze over, but that is another story.

*

At one point, my mother thought Havard and I would grow old together. We bought a Honda Civic. We rented a Happy Camper van and toured Iceland, bathing in geothermal pools and waterfalls. We took photos of Skógafoss; the falling water sounded like thunder, and the mist formed double rainbows. We were, she believed, a binary system, two stars in an eternal orbit, gravitationally bound to each other.

Outside my mother's celestial fantasy, Havard was a commercial photographer, but his hobby was buying items at thrift shops and reselling them on Kijiji. Sometimes, he convinced himself he had use for the item and sometimes he planned, from the point of purchase, to make a profit. Once in a while, he struck second-hand gold. He found for $3.99 an old Leica IIIf someone had mistaken for a point-and-shoot. He asked $600, took $550, and we bought an all-season tent.

Havard did not view the sales as a mere business transaction. Part of the appeal was the engagement, the interaction with strangers, who in Havard's mind, became his friends. Havard stretched out each sale, searching for common interests. "'Record in a Bag?' No kidding! I have all of Hollerado's albums!" He exchanged email addresses and chatted for months about the vintage amp that he sold to his ersatz soulmate from Meat Cove.

"I think it's nice," my mother said too emphatically. "I think it's nice that he does normal things."

I tell my friend Veronika that I want the memory-erasing pill, which is, I believe, a form of beta blocker. The things that keep me awake are not the bad things that others have done; they are my poorly thought-out actions made in *those* moments.

Veronika is sitting in my living room and she is impossible to ignore. Her body language, the way she deliberately spreads her arms when talking, drawing attention to the negative space around her. These are things I have started to notice. She is disturbing all the air around her and she really, really shouldn't. *You should know by now*, I think, *that I need things still.*

Veronika is an indie clothing designer who makes cotton tunics with asymmetrical shoulders. Today, she is that perfect splash of colour in the monochromatic backdrop of my room. The lone pigment. She is wearing a mustard-coloured jumpsuit made from crumpled fabric. It ends mid-calf. She could have been coloured by a digital artist with Photoshop, a magician who turns models into mermaids with luminescent fins.

"Is this because of Jack?" she asks, and I catch her staring at my hands like she has never seen them before. *I hate it when you do that.*

"Jack Jack Jack." I repeat the name as though I am tired of hearing her say it.

"Jack's a fuckboy."

"No, he's not."

You don't understand, I think. *It's complicated.*

In my family, we ignore the elephants in the room; we give people time to collect their belongings, turn off the lights, and escape. Veronika, who cannot keep her arms still like she should, pokes the elephant with her umbrella, and then, once the pachyderm is disturbed, plows forward, nonplussed.

"Some group that measures things like that claims that the Danes are the happiest people in the world," Veronika says. She pretends she wasn't staring but I saw her, just like I saw her staring at the shoes in my entranceway, seeing who they belonged to. "Maybe that's because of the memory-erasing pill."

"Maybe," I allow.

I tell Veronika that I once sat in the middle of a group of Danes at an international paddling regatta, and they were, for the most part, odd. They reminded me of children on a class outing—one could not do anything without the others. If one got up for a snack, they all got up, annoying the rows around them. They had blankets and red-and-white jester hats and tins of baked goods, which they passed back and forth, and they were, I suppose, happy, until a Danish paddler stopped before the finish line, and one man started to cry.

"Did he actually cry?" she asks.

Over her head is a metal sculpture — six stems of dark wire shooting from an invisible earth, branches devoid of buds and leaves — and it is as weightless as my story about the crying Dane. I am getting tired of the sculpture, I have just decided. It is too dark, too bleak.

"Yes, he did," I reply. "And it was sad because he was one of the younger ones. And he looked pitiful. He had bad skin and he seemed slow."

"And he cried?"

"Yes. He was sobbing."

She gives me *that look*, the one that tells me that her brain is working too hard for her delicate head. It's the same look that people give me when they learn that I am pursuing a PhD — "What will you do with it?" But that is a pointless question, like asking the pilgrim on the eight-hundred-mile trek along the historic California Mission Trail, "Why?" It's where I am right now, halfway down the trail; it is where I am.

Havard had some annoying habits. He would, without fail, drop all of his camera bags, lenses, and tripods in the living room as soon as he came home, and it was the first room anyone viewed upon entering, a room that I tried to make hospitable. Havard was not happy unless his possessions were on shambolic display. He had to see them and smell them the moment he entered. The big-screen TV. His fixed-gear bicycle. His "special" hiking boots. All evidence he existed.

"Can we please move the hockey bag into the basement?" I once asked.

"What? And get everything mouldy?"

I sighed, and he countered with, "Did you touch my bike?"

"No," I said. "You said you would move it from the living room—"

"I will," he lied. "I will."

•

> Ivy Tanner was particularly proud of her first real job, working as a smartly dressed waitress in the elegant dining room of Yarmouth's original Grand Hotel. She never put her needs above those of her children and grandchildren, and in their adoring eyes, Ivy was a provider, a forgiver, and a saint. Ivy loved the colour turquoise and all pretty things. Despite his many flaws, Ivy always loved Fuzzy, and despite himself, he surely truly knew it.

I think my favourite section of my thesis is the one that contains tributes celebrating people who lived, on the surface, the most ordinary of lives, individuals like Ivy or Max or Henry.

> Many will remember Max as the raspberry guy, who greeted everyone with a smile and a box of berries. He has now been promoted to glory to be with his Lord and Saviour.

> Henry loved his Mi'kmaw language, culture, and community. He took great pride in being part of the annual Moose Harvest with the youth camp.

Veronika thinks that I am immersed in obituaries because I am trying to understand myself. She thinks I am trying to decide what makes a prodigious life and what a bad one, that I am trying to determine how many mistakes one can make and still be loved. And if this is true, I have not yet found the answer.

Not all of Havard's Kijiji sales went smoothly. Once, after he advertised an air conditioner, a family of four showed up at our door, English their second language. When Havard told them the price was $120, they collectively waved their hands down. *Lower lower*, as though they had rehearsed it.

"Okay, this is the best I can do," said Havard, not used to such intense negotiations with such a concerted force. "I can give it to you for ninety dollars."

"Can you say eighty-four?" asked the mother. "That's our lucky number."

Havard sighed, "Okay."

Havard looked down, and the younger girl, who

appeared about six, was trying to hold his hand. He managed to extricate himself without anyone taking notice, and when the mother rifled through her purse for bills, Havard reminded her of the price.

"Can you say seventy-five?"

"You said eight-four was your lucky number."

She just stared back.

If I had to describe Havard, I would say that he was a watercolour painted in traditional English style with a palette of four or five colours, setting—at best—a tone of mystery and gloom. Now, add square black glasses. And on risqué days, a grey beanie. Havard was one of those men who had always had a girlfriend, the guy who went to prom with the cute girl in the sparkly white dress whose parents took photos. Havard was rattled by the family, which did not give him their email address or become his pretend friends. But he was—like a boy who was never without a girlfriend—undeterred. He was back selling three nights later.

"Hey." His tone was upbeat.

From the bedroom, I heard Havard escort someone in. I crept into the hallway from where I could see a young man wearing a vintage green Bavarian Alps hat with a feather. *Do I know him?* I asked myself, uncertain. *The face*—

"Wow, it looks great," I heard him say.

Havard was showing the visitor a dark-brown ukulele he had picked up for forty dollars. They were hunched over the instrument, which had twenty fret wires and nylon strings "that might need replacing."

"I like the fact that it is so worn," said the customer.

"Oh yeah," said Havard. "It has character, but as you can see there is no splitting or cracking." He turned the instrument over for inspection.

"No, it looks good, man."

"Did you ever watch the video of IZ Kamakawiwoʻole playing 'Over the Rainbow'?" asked Havard.

"That is why I wanted to take up ukulele!" The customer looked like he could explode from happiness, he looked like Havard had just seen into his heart and it was still young and unbroken by life. "I cry every time I watch it, man, every single time—"

Havard's overly exuberant customer stayed for twenty minutes, and Havard offered him a cappuccino. They drank their coffees and settled on a price of seventy dollars. Carrying case included. Havard walked the customer to the street, where they continued to talk. I returned to the bedroom and picked up a book to appear as though I had been reading.

"I like that guy." Havard appeared in the doorway, money in hand. "He's a student at your school. I mentioned your name and he says he knows who you are."

"Oh. What's his name?"

"Cosmo. He said he's a friend of Jack's. Who is Jack?"

And just like that, the cat was out of the proverbial bag.

•

The most nostalgic section of my thesis is the one that contains old names no longer in common usage. I spend hours with those names and sometimes I have conversations with people named Leander and Toss and I imagine we are in a country kitchen with a daybed and a cast-iron woodstove covered in nickel and the air is both warm and damp.

I have a total of 409 old names that I have classified as uncommonly dated, including Loman, Alricha, Minnie, Halden, Alton, Niva, Effie, Fayreen, Obediah, Medford, Rufus, and Ivy.

> Augustus Whitman lived to the age of 100 because he was lucky. He had not lived a more abstemious life than others. He had not cross-country skied across gorges like the allegorical 60-year-old Swede, stopping at the end of the day for a Thermos of coffee and biscuits. He hadn't given up salt. Augustus had not exercised his brain by learning Mandarin in his golden years. Nothing unusual had happened to Augustus when he was a young man: no extraordinary riches or success. This was his luck, a body that had not broken down at 300,000 kilometres and a mind that had not stopped working like a cellphone dropped in the sink. Augustus claimed that he used up all his luck when he met his wife, Alberta, in 1938, but he was wrong.

I also have 228 nicknames that speak to the character of the people and their birthplace (Fluff, Buckaroo, So Long, Duckie, Fuzzy.) In some parts of the province, nicknames were not given affectionately and were used as a means of torment. No one, I propose, asked to be called Pie Face MacNeil or Aluminum Leg Gable, but they were.

What can I tell you about Jack without making myself sound fatuous and foolish? If Havard was an English watercolour, then Jack was a pop art painting by Lichtenstein. Jack had the ability to fix you with his eyes and persuade you to join him in a secret bond—a nebulous never-defined meeting of the minds, a collision of the souls—that you then believed had to happen.

Jack was blond and sun-drenched. Twenty-two. His checkered shirt looked in danger of flying off. He had a speech bubble over his yellow head that said, "Hey!" and you could never be blamed because you were doing nothing to propel these events. You were doing nothing but showing up at class and waiting for him to raise his hand, your TA's heart racing, and you weren't even sure it was happening, were you?

One section of my thesis shows how families obliquely convey the cause of death: Donations may be made to the Mental Health Society, or Anthony Recovery House, the Liver Association, or Daisy's Women's Shelter. And so it goes, a wall of good intentions demolished by the randomness of life, which does not discriminate between sinners and saints.

People who die from the effects of alcoholism are often described as: "Albert was a very social person who enjoyed fishing and had a love for animals." Suicides are "sudden deaths" and sometimes the suddenness is expected, and at other times so unpredicted, so cataclysmic, that it can never be processed. "Shaun was too sensitive for this world. He will be remembered for his gentle spirit. In lieu of donations, reach out to someone before they are swallowed by darkness." And I can see Shaun, someone's much-loved son and beautiful brother. If he was still here, he would tell you that no one asks to be a poet or a paper ballerina.

Havard changed his phone number and his email address after I moved out. He ghosted me, and so I waited until I saw a Kijiji ad and I replied as dawna234@hotmail.com. The ad was for a sixteen-by-twenty Saunders Omega darkroom easel and he was asking $120. I knew it was Havard because, even though he had a new email, I had been there when he found that easel for $10. Havard and dawna234 exchanged messages, and I went to his house.

"What do you want?" he asked, knowing the answer.

"Ahhhh." I thought about saying something.

I wanted to apologize for running off with Jack, I suppose. I wanted to make it right, but Havard didn't care because he wasn't hurting anymore. I was. I wasn't seeking to comfort him; I was seeking absolution for myself. And then—as he stood there holding his ten-dollar easel and looking, for all the world, like a bad idea—I decided, *Screw this*. And I left.

•

In obituaries, I have found, in addition to tributes, cruelty and potshots. People use the submissions to settle scores—

"Abandoned by his mother, Darrell had a very hard life"—or to rewrite a life story that should not have been rewritten, an offence most common among second or third wives in control of the body and, for one day, the past.

> Dean's life began when he met the Love of His Life Barb and her son, Dwight. They enjoyed many wonderful hours at the Windsor Curling Club and at their retirement village in Florida, where they made great friends. He is also survived by his ex-wife and eight children.

Did you know that Kierkegaard and Andersen are buried in the same cemetery, and that people can say whatever they want about you after you are dead? Someone wrote a play about Andersen and masturbation. Someone else alleged that he had stalked Dickens, and that the little match girl didn't need to die, and who, I might ask, gets to be the judge of that? The same people who believe that life is easy?

People can sit in a room with you every day and lie, people you adore. People who neglected to tell you that they were—while you were editing their papers and slow-roasting Mexican pork for dinner—apartment shopping two days in a row. Checking out futons. After you saw them out the door with, "Have a great day. Love you."

And you were not surprised when Jack ran away with Heide after just three months. She was so bright and shiny and lissome that you knew it was supposed to be, in the same way that the ugly duckling was supposed to turn into a swan. Heide was a piece of wedding cake, butter-filled and divine, left on your plate after your third glass of wine, impossible, at that point, to resist. And you were both moving forward in your own way weren't you? Both figuring out who you were supposed to be.

It is a week since Veronika visited me and brought up Jack. Things have changed.

She just broke up with a waiter named Igor, who looked like Íñigo Melchor Fernández de Velasco, the Spanish nobleman whose portrait hung in the Louvre. Igor had long black hair parted in the middle, a pencil moustache, and a wide-brimmed hat. And after a while, it had become tedious—*the look*—people noticing him everywhere. "Oh look. Igor the waiter." Like so many things in life, Veronika tells me, it got old. *Plus the fact that he is a cheater*, I think, but say instead, "I can see that. Havard got old."

Kierkegaard once asked: "What is a poet? An unhappy person who conceals profound anguish in his heart but whose lips are so formed that as sighs and cries pass over them they sound like beautiful music."

If you are manning the Gates of Heaven, you have met Kierkegaard and judged him. But here is what you need to know about me: Havard didn't "believe" in birthday presents; his strewn belongings were passive-aggressive weapons in an undeclared war; Havard's mother was a big bossy woman who took up too much space.

Charlie—her real name was Charlene, but she called herself Charlie to create the illusion of youthfulness and fun—was the type of woman who would show up at a sporting event with a lawn chair and park herself in front of everyone, chin cocked like Donald Trump. So that you would say to yourself, *Oh dear. There she is.*

Have you ever driven to a wilderness park with a slender path through the woods—over rocks and tricky stumps—and arrived at a glorious cliff overlooking the ocean? And there is, for that moment, nothing but history and air, and your body is lifted by the negative ions, and you feel freedom. Charlie had the opposite effect. She was a one-woman atmospheric condition, killing the mood. And she hated me.

She hated the back tattoo I got when I was twenty during my first round of SSRIs.

And the sleeve I got at twenty-three, terrified by visions too awful to share, so I won't.

She hated the constellation on my right hand that I turned to each morning, seeking direction, when my life was a cacophony of bad decisions and fear.

And it is the fear that I most want to forget, the fear that comes from being so ill that you hide razors under your pillow and you hurt yourself to feel better pain.

Havard's mother hated the fact that I was damaged even when I was better. When I had weathered the storms and come through as resilient as Ivy filling water glasses in the Grand Hotel, loving a man who did his best to dissuade her. She hated the scars I had covered with ink, and every time I saw her, I could see the judgment in her eyes, and after a while I saw it in Havard's eyes, too.

> Shaun was the son every mother wished for, the brother you would have chosen. He was the kindest sweetest boy who ever walked this Earth and we will miss him every single day.

If you could touch sadness, your hand would go right through it—it would have no heat, no pulse or texture, nothing you could truly feel. If you could smell sadness, it would smell like the coldest bleakest day of fall, the day when the trees are stripped and the sun has deserted you, and there are wet slippery puddles of grief on the ground pretending to be leaves. If you could hear sadness, it would sound like tears.

One day, I looked in my closet and realized that everything was black—the black of death, the black of despair, the black of cynics and nihilists with shrivelled-up souls. The black of people with dialled-down emotions and hearts that have, through suffering, been turned to mute. When Havard and I were in Iceland we came upon a public chalk board and it said, *Before I Die I Want to*... and someone wrote, *live free*, and someone wrote, *make it*, and someone wrote, *meet David Hasselhoff*, and I wrote nothing.

And so, last week, I purchased a pair of slim turquoise pants, tight at the ankles and so exuberant that they smiled when I tried them on. They were the turquoise that you might find on a vintage car or a sari woven with real silver and real gold.

•

> In lieu of flowers, Keith would ask that you be good and stay out of trouble.

•

I tell Veronika that I am thinking of adopting a dog now that I am better. And it will be the happiest, most free dog you have ever met, and I will let him do whatever he wants. I will take him swimming in the lake and throw him sticks, and when he comes home, he can lie in the middle of the floor where Jack's backpack used to be and he can be full of mud for all I care. He can smell like moss and muck. And I will buy him toys and I will buy myself a Ford truck and he can sit up front and stick his head out the window. And maybe I will name him Buckaroo or Rufus or Slink because that is a good thing to do, the right thing to do, the thing that makes the most people happy, and maybe, just maybe, we won't even go to Denmark. And maybe I will surely truly love him.

Rafael Has Pretty Eyes

"I had a friend who graduated from J-school, and the only work she can get is selling stories online. They have to be salacious, shocking, and filled with gratuitous swear words."

> *John Dalrymple, sixty-nine, may look like an average Canadian senior with a head of white hair and a rumpled cardigan with butter stains, but the truth may surprise you. John—not his real name—is actually Nova Scotia's most infamous Furry. "Hell, yes," says John.*

Whenever the two sisters meet, Maggie, the older one, talks in loquacious bursts, as though she is being paid by the word.

"That's bad," says Ella.

"Whatever." Maggie tosses the word into the air, a handful of nonchalance.

"Is the friend *you*?" asks Ella, six years younger.

"Maybe."

*

"What are we doing about food?"

"Falafel?"

"It was closed yesterday."

"Canada Day," declares Maggie, "the saddest day of the year. When all of the rich people flock to their cottages on the ocean and hoist gigantic flags and the poor people flood the streets, an army of scavengers in search of a free piece of cake."

"Did you see the fireworks?"

"They were okay."

"Who'd you go with?"

"Andy and his friend Luke."

"Okay."

"He's a Brit. Always saying stuff like 'dirty knacker scum' and 'wanker.' Once, he said, 'I'd beat him around the block a few times.'"

"Sounds annoying."

"He is. Can't believe one of my friends hooked up with him."

"Was it you?"

"Maybe."

A man sits across from the sisters in the tiny restaurant, which has six tables and windows overlooking the street. Vainly thin, the man has a lush head of white hair that allows him to effortlessly wear jeans and a casual sweater. Toms. He could be a weekend sailor or a collector of vintage cars; he could have a younger wife or a wife his age who feels frumpy.

The girls give the man a look, and then Ella asks, "You still house-sitting?"

Ella is in that stage where you try on personas, hoping for a fit: Rebel. Artist. Jock. Anime. Geek. Not that long ago, she wore a soccer uniform with the top tucked in, a dorky green sweatband. A poufy grade-nine prom dress with untameable tulle.

"Yeah," says Maggie. "They have a fridge that plays music."

Now Ella has a pierced lip and mauve hair.

"Their dog is nice and they're both profs," says Maggie, who wears Dragon Girl red lipstick. "Well, she's a prof; he's gone. She told me: 'In case you are curious, my husband ran off with a forty-year-old twit who teaches Jacobean drama because young people *really* care about that.' And she talks in literary tropes."

"I don't know—"

"Me neither."

"Wish I could get a dog."

"A dog would be good for you. Look, there's Rafael outside on the sidewalk with his boyfriend. Rafael has the prettiest eyes. He wears liner, but it works on him because his eyes are so pretty."

The white-haired man is wearing a chest carrier shaped like a Snugli. Striped, it has four leg holes filled by four white legs. The man acts as though it is normal, reading the menu with a tiny white dog on his chest, a dog with black buttons for a nose, eyes, and mouth. A dog that sticks out its tongue repeatedly.

"Okay. He is FaceTiming me," Maggie says.

"Who?"

"Luke."

She hits the mute button on her phone.

"He told me he didn't mean to sound 'ratty.'"

"Is he, like, a soccer hooligan?"

"I don't know. He needs to stop FaceTiming me, he needs to stop calling everyone 'a dirty wanker.'"

A woman joins the man who is wearing the dog carrier. It is clear from the way she is perched at the table—too upright, too energized—that they are not an old married couple. He assumes an air of nonchalance; she leans forward and slaps the table whenever he says something slightly funny. *Slap. Ha ha. Slap.* Each slap straight from the tips of her pointed navy blue shoes.

"Did you really interview a Furry?"

"Sort of. I'm selling them a piece now on adoptees who find their birth mothers and have sex. It happens more often than you would think. It's called *consanguinamorous* something—"

"Gross."

"Cousin marriage is legal in Canada by the way, but I am not talking about that—"

"Okay."

"I am talking about people who didn't know each other before."

"Still gross—"

"It's a psychological thing. It's not their fault."

Ella keeps her eyes on her phone, as though that is her job.

Her arms and legs are still growing; they are as long and slim as her favourite gel pen, the purple one that leaves an inscrutable trail. For her birthday, Maggie had given her a new pack of gel pens and a journal with *Love Dance Care Dream* repeated on the cover.

"How's school?" asks Maggie.

"Okay," says Ella, who does not know she will never be this unfinished, this fleeting, again.

"Glad I'm done."

"Lucky."

"My old roommate is in Thailand teaching English. Remember Kyra? She went through an Emily Dickinson phase only wearing white. It was an act though. She wasn't too sensitive for the outside world and she only wrote one poem and it was awful."

"I don't know who—"

"Doesn't matter. She's one of those people who buys a lion-mane wig for her dog and expects everyone to like it."

"Okay. Annoying."

"Did you know that before the war only ten per cent of Canadians went to university, and then it became *de rigueur*, and everyone went and it was fine until the jobs ran out. And then they lost the boys."

"What do you mean?"

"They flunked out, went to Fort Mac, joined the army—"

"What about Kevin?"

"No. Kevin was good at school if by 'good' you mean 'deranged.' He gave his mom's dog chocolate *in an experiment*"—she puts the words in air quotes—"to see if would *kill* him."

"Didn't she own an Escalade?"

"Yeah. We drove it to Maine that time, and it was sick."

"Really?"

"Arguably the best weekend of my life."

•

Ella watches the man pop a piece of chicken into the dog's mouth. It is clear by now that bringing a small animal to lunch is not a good idea, but he is committed. Committed to eating his chicken kebabs while carrying a six-pound dog that stares plaintively at diners with its tongue stuck out. The woman slaps the table. *Ha ha. Who knows the truth about anyone?* Ella thinks. What they might do. Their secret wishes.

"I did something the other day *you* should do," claims Maggie. "I got on the bus and sat next to the weirdest person there. There were empty seats. But I picked an old hippy woman with synthetic pink hair stuck in her bun like Easter decorations."

"Okay."

Ella glances at the laughing woman, who reminds her of her former math teacher, the nice one who took her to the hospital when she broke her arm in gym and stayed when no one showed up. When that nurse was mean and asked her questions she shouldn't have.

"She told me she got depressed when her kids left home.

She said she had a choice. She could sit there and wallow, play Ray LaMontagne songs. Watch that scene from *The Champ* where Jon Voight plays the dying boxer, with Ricky Schroder as his son, determined, by someone, to be the saddest movie scene ever. Little Ricky crying 'Wake up, Champ' and acting his heart out."

"I don't know who—"

"Doesn't matter."

"Okay."

"Champ dies, by the way."

"Okay."

"Or she could shake it off. Do something fun. Put on a Zac Efron movie. Paint her bedroom robin's egg blue. Eat Laura Secord white chocolate. She could excuse herself for making the mistake of thinking that her kids would always be there and she would always be happy."

"Did this really happen?"

"Maybe."

•

The sisters finish lunch.

"Well, I'm going to meet him," announces Maggie, who has been on her phone.

"Who?"

"Luke."

"Show me a picture."

"Here."

"Yeah, he's cute. Looks like Zayn Malik."

"Yes, that's *exactly* what I thought!"

"Zayn has sad eyes."

"Luke said he's over here because the gypsies ruined the sink estates where the poor people live. And they are mean to animals. He said they wouldn't have that problem in Norway. In Norway, any child who shows anti-social behaviour—aggression or animal abuse—is taken away and put somewhere until they can behave like a normal human being."

"What happens if they don't?"

"Dunno. Maybe they kill them."

"Is that true?"

"Yes."

"I thought they were nice in Norway."

"Apparently not."

The sisters drift to the counter to pay. On the way, they pass the non-couple and the white dog and give them a sideways look. Ella moves the way young girls move, protecting herself with hunched shoulders, circling life until the world has a place for her to land, a place where she is wanted.

They walk to a bus stop, Maggie towering over her sister.

"Do *not* tell Mom *any* of this." Maggie issues the order abruptly. "Do not tell her about Luke. Do not tell that we visited Dad and his new girlfriend. And do *not* tell her about my Furry story or she will think it is about Bruce."

"I hate Bruce," Ella says, eyes on the sidewalk.

"He's so stupid."

"I wish he was dead."

"Don't say that around Mom either."

"He's there all the time."

"Try to ignore him."

Their time together over, Maggie remembers her role, the one she was *supposed* to play, and so she demands, "Do you have your bus pass?"

"Yes."

"You're okay getting home?"

"YES!"

"Are you sure?

"YES!"

The sidewalk is so crowded that people are moving en masse as though they are on a conveyer belt being shifted from one airport terminal to another, their feet invisible, a blur of backs and backpacks, a faceless progression.

Maggie leaves Ella at the Plexiglas bus shelter. And Ella is not thinking about the bus. She is thinking about *her:* the most beautiful girl in the world. A girl who smelled like strawberries. Next to her, she felt awkward and ugly. She was the type of girl who did not need a mirror because everything had been perfectly arranged for her: her eyes, her hair, the way her jeans hung over her perfect hips, and it was that nonchalance that tricked Ella. It tricked her into thinking that maybe the girl did not know how perfect she was and maybe she might love Ella for who she was.

"Love you."

And before long the bus will come and go without Ella, and no one will know where she has gone. The missing-persons report will give her height and age and hair colour: mauve. And that's the way it happens some of the time, not *always*, but some of the time. With unseen girls like Ella. Other times it happens for no reason, as though a malevolent god with time on his hands decides to break someone's heart, to hurl a of bolt of tragedy into the midst of a model family, to make them feel foolish for ever celebrating anything good in their lives.

"Love you, too."

We Were Lucky

This is the story of boys and how they break their mother's hearts.

When I was a boy, I had a best friend named Bobby who lived one street over. The summer we turned eleven, my neighbours rented their basement to a childless couple. The man was in the navy. The wife liked to lie out in the backyard on a blanket while wearing a two-piece bathing suit with purple and yellow daisies. Sometimes, she had a transistor radio, and then one day, Mister Thompson, the boarder who lived upstairs, a tall man with a brush cut the colour of bulrushes, joined her, and everything became peculiar.

Bang. Bang. Bang.

My mother opened our door, hiding, as she always did, our family's life behind her.

"Could you ask your children to stop invading my privacy?" It was the wife from the basement in a white sleeveless top and slacks. Back then, when Pontiac Parisiennes were the rage, when *Singalong Jubilee* was on the air, women wore their hair in stiff sprayed helmets and hers was taupe.

"What do you mean?" asked my mother, rubbing her hands on the cotton housedress she wore for cleaning.

"They are spying on me."

"Well, I can't imagine that they—"

Bobby and I stayed out of sight. We weren't at that stage yet, that powerless stage, where the mere proximity of a woman disarmed us.

"Well, they are."

I remember that the woman owned a Singer sewing machine, which she had set up in the one basement window that got sunlight. I remember that the boarder was lanky, but not the lanky of a compulsive runner or a health nut, the lanky of a man who came that way. I remember that a boy from my school had fallen off a pier that same week and drowned while fishing for mackerel.

"I will talk to my husband—"

My mother closed the door and said nothing to me or Bobby—we had been heading to my room with a bottle of grasshoppers. I waited for my mother to mention the woman, but she said nothing. I waited for her to absolve me of blame or to tell me that the woman, who had been flaunting her liaison, was out of line. Her silence sounded like the low hum of an aging freezer.

•

Our North End neighbourhood was working class—there was a dump, a prison, a slaughterhouse. We didn't know that people owned yachts; we didn't know that they went to Europe when there wasn't a war. My grandmother had lost an eye in the Explosion—she always seemed to have a hanky pressed to her face—and we had relatives who had been raised in an orphanage. We were, my mother told us, lucky.

I had two older sisters; Bobby was the middle kid in a family of eight. The first kids in both families were expected to excel at everything, charting a safe navigable course for the others. Bobby and I were more free. We got into rock fights. We raided a neighbour's garden, ripping up beets and carrots we wouldn't eat if you paid us. We stole twenty cents from a milk bottle left on a step.

"Let's go to the dump," I said that day, a day when something happened.

"Sure."

"The back way so they don't see us."

There was one kid in school I hated and if I saw him today, I'd probably still hate him. His name was Jamie and he couldn't let you have anything. Most people have the ability to be happy if their own needs are satisfied, and then there are the others. The people who could not let you have anything: a hobby, a pet, a write-up in the newspaper. And it might be the only thing you had that mattered, the only thing you looked forward to each day.

If Jamie had eight friends and he noticed that you had one, he would try to take that friend from you. He would invite him to his birthday, he would lend him a baseball glove, and once he had stolen your friend, he wouldn't give a shit. He tried to steal Bobby, but Bobby said Jamie was a "dirty bugger."

"You never told Jamie nothin'?" I asked.

"No way."

"You didn't tell him about the gun, did you?"

"Do you think I'm stupid?"

To get to the dump the long way, we had to pass a corner store that sold penny candy and Popsicles, whole or broken in half. It was run by a "foreign" man named Al, who would, word went, "rip you off." Al seemed small, dark, and mysterious.

"I don't know for sure," I said. "I just heard my father say 'a gun.' I am pretty sure he said 'the dump'—"

"Probably."

"There was radioactive stuff there from the hospital before. It could have blown up everything."

"That would be bad."

Back then, your days had a beginning and an end, and when you turned off your light, it was just you and a Hardy Boys book you had hidden under your bed. Life had not yet sped up, your internal clock altered by an incessant flow of information, as relentless and confusing as the midnight sun. Back then, you did not discover, until the following day, that anything had happened. You had time for pointless pursuits.

I thought about the woman and the boarder as Bobby and I crossed town. I wondered if his brush cut felt like bulrushes, velvety but rough, before you soaked them in kerosene and set them on fire. I wondered if the navy man would catch him and beat him up like John Wayne in a classic movie fist fight. If that happened, I wanted to be there.

We passed our teacher's house. Mrs. Harris. She was nice enough. We had a class of thirty-five, including one boy who had "water on the brain" and one girl who'd had scarlet fever. A boy with German parents had the mockable last name of Bierwagen, and we wouldn't let him play War with us. "Go home," we'd shout. "You dirty Kraut."

There was another class for the worse-off kids, the ones without fathers or half a chance. One boy in grade five drove a taxi and he brought it to school. Frankie Williams was from Africville, and he saved me when a bully tried to beat me up. Then his house got bulldozed when they buried the whole place.

"Just jump the fence," Bobby ordered.

The first thing that hit you was the smell. Like something toxic was burning. There was a guard on the dump entrance, which is why we jumped.

I trusted that my father knew what was what. He watched the TV news. Sometimes, he looked at a weekly run by a man from the States, but he wasn't crazy about it. The American had moved to Nova Scotia because he didn't like things at home and then found fault with everything here. Sometimes my father called him a "four flusher." He used names like that, ones you never hear today: Shorty Montego and Toughie Hot Stuff. My father was a good father but he couldn't spend all his time worrying about small stuff. He'd been to war. So badly injured that he'd been anointed for death, which my mother told me in *that* voice, the one that assumed I understand the gravity of the words—*anointed for death*—when, in fact, I didn't.

My mother was one of *those* mothers, who tried—she tried with every ounce of her tiny being. People like my mother couldn't afford to be frivolous; they couldn't drive through life with the top down. They were born stoic and guarded. My mother took pride in ironed clothes and homemade birthday cakes, and you had the feeling she would never give up no matter how bad it got.

The dump was stacked high with old fridges, heaters, and *Star Weekly* magazines, compressed, the newest on top. Bobby found some wood we could use for a buggy. "All we need is wheels." Jamie had a fancy buggy that his brother made. Having an older brother put Jamie at an advantage—he knew about cars and buggies and *Playboy*. His brother was a greaser who drove a '54 Meteor. Years later, Jamie's brother went to Vietnam and nobody knew why.

"Where do you think they found it?"

"Probably near the back."

We looked up.

A truck had pulled up and was unloading junk. A man was throwing boxes into a pile, everything flying like it had been caught by a giant fan.

"It could have been an army gun."

We didn't see the other man until it was too late to hide.

"What you boys looking for?"

"Ahh nothin'."

Last week, my mother was cleaning out her basement, and I went over to help. When I stepped through the door, I felt caught in the middle of a fight between my memory and my conscience. There are so many times in life when you can lie — to yourself and others — about the choices you have made. And then there are times when lying is as pointless as throwing sand into the wind.

It had been five years since my father passed, and the house felt too big and too small at the same time. On one end table was a framed photo of my father I had never seen before — him as a young boy with a white ceramic dog. Did it belong to him, I wondered, the dog, or did it belong to the photographer? My mother had placed a vase of mixed flowers on another table, and I wondered if someone had given them to her. They looked like something she wouldn't buy for herself.

When I left home after high school, I ticked off every box on my mother's disappointment list. I dropped out of college. I got arrested at a sit-in. I lived on a commune in northern Ontario that grew weed and dirty children. I joined the Children of God. Took acid. Had a child she never met. I was, you could say, living in the moment and that moment was a very weird and disconnected one; it was a moment that had had nothing before it and nothing after; it was the single cardboard-mounted slide inserted in a projector, the colours saturated and intense, sharper than a print.

Bobby married a girl from high school and bought the house next door to his in-laws.

I followed my mother into the basement, and behind the furnace we found a box of black-and-white school photos. Tall kids in the back, shorter ones seated in front. Back then for photos, boys wore bow ties, white shirts, and slicked-back hair; girls, their best dresses. Bobby wore an oversized grin, but it never looked real. I stood on my toes to seem taller.

On the backs of my class photos, my mother had written the names of the students. "Do you want these?" She placed the pictures on a chair with an indifference that surprised me.

In a shoebox, my mother had saved my *Baby's First Christmas* cards, my confirmation certificate, my report cards. I opened my grade three report card and I tried to remember *that* time. I could remember putting pennies on the train tracks. Collecting chestnuts and making a weapon using a drill and shoelaces —

1st Qtr: John's work is untidy.

2nd Qtr: John wastes his time.

3rd Qtr: John still wastes his time, but there is hope for improvement.

We went upstairs, and in an attempt to make amends for something, I asked my mother about Mrs. Harris. My mother said my old teacher had a sad routine. Every day the widow walked down a hill and waited at a bus stop for her first ride to the Casino. One night, in a blizzard, she stood there in a raccoon coat from the seventies and she seemed confused, as though she wasn't sure what to do, but could not stop. Her children "never bothered with her," my mother added with what may have been a look.

When I was young, my mother had the brightest blue eyes — it was a colour that held you in its grip — but I noticed then how the pigment had faded, just like the pigment in her auburn hair. It was as though her body was slowly withdrawing from life, becoming more passive, more invisible, more mute. That intense blue, it was the thing I had always noticed, the thing that made her special.

I needed to think about something else, so I asked my mother as we sat in the living room, curtains drawn, TV blaring with a show she never watched, "What nationality was Al, the corner-store man?"

"He was French. From Quebec."

"Really?"

"Why, yes."

"What happened to that man from church with the scarred face? Was it an explosion?"

"No, he had cancer."

"What about those people who lived next door in the basement. That woman with the sewing machine. You know—he was in the navy."

"Oh, them."

"Yes, you know—"

"Oh, they were nothing special."

It wasn't the answer I wanted; it felt too slim, too offhand, as though it diminished the import of everything that happened that summer. And so I told my mother that I used spy on the woman and that I left her a note that said: "You will go to hell." I placed a rotten tomato on her windowsill. And after I saw her and Mister Thompson drinking beer and hiding their empties under the step, we stole the empties—me and Bobby—and maybe my mother heard me and maybe she didn't because she shrugged, as though to say, "Who cares?"

My mother walked into the kitchen and she stared into the yard where my father used to build a skating rink in winter, believing I would one day make the NHL. She stared so long that I think she saw him, watering the rink at midnight, bundled up in an army surplus coat and a toque. He worked two jobs and he didn't own a car and he had nightmares that woke him up, screaming. Sudden noises startled him so terribly, so deeply, that he cursed and then said, the way he'd been taught, "Lord, forgive me for swearing." And there was a divide back then—as clear as the line between the posh South End and the blue-collar North where people concealed their missing eyes—either your father had been to war or he hadn't, and there were kids in the neighbourhood with younger dads or dads who had somehow missed it, and things were easier for them. They just were.

"And what about that shooting?" I had followed my mother to the kitchen. "You know." As though it was finally safe to talk about it, the battles between us now won and lost.

"I guess he just wasn't right," she said, her voice as flat as a freshly ironed dress shirt laid out for a class photo. And then, exasperated, "*Who knows* why he did it!"

But he did do it, didn't he? On an ordinary August evening when boys were playing War and riding bikes. Going to the dump to look for an imaginary gun. A teenager on a bicycle came right up to them and he shot them one by one: three boys the same age as me and Bobby. One was picking blueberries, one standing outside a corner store, one heading home from sailing. That's how I remember it anyway.

People stayed inside their houses for two days until the cops found the shooter near the airport. It was all over the news. The American wrote a column saying that it was the end of our innocence, just like when Lee Harvey Oswald shot JFK in Dallas. And my father—well I can't remember what my father said because there were things he never talked about, things he avoided, in the same way that he couldn't go to funerals or hospitals to see people, so my mother went for them both. The way he never entered a Legion, but cried quiet heartbroken tears when anyone died. The way he hid his navy tattoos. The long fine crack in his skull. And like most careless boys I assumed that my mother loved me more than anyone in the world, including him, and maybe I was wrong.

The Rakin Bus

Harold Fox picked a fine day to ride the bus.

The city councillor was seated behind Ronnie Snooks, the local rep for the drivers' union. Ronnie had a creepy-clown tattoo on his forearm, and his grey hair was agitated as though it had come around the corner in its underwear and found an intruder in the house.

"This driver used to be on the coastal run," a transit spokesperson told Harold with an implicit stare. "We are optermistic that the 99 is a good fit for him."

As a politician, Harold was used to pretending he knew things he didn't—faces, names, why all the side windows of the bus were covered in black—and so he pretended that he knew about the "coastal run," which was actually "a low-stress rehabilitative route for drivers." He pretended the spokesperson had not said "optermistic."

Harold's seat was elevated like a throne, facing the door, and he nodded when an octogenarian hobbled on. The man had a cumulous cloud of white hair, which gave him an angelic air, not that you could mention angels around seniors—Harold had made that mistake once. The old man wore Steampunk glasses he didn't know were Steampunk.

"Isn't Ride-a-Bus Day terrific?" Harold asked with his usual pep.

Because he had never been on this bus before, Harold didn't know that the senior was a regular *and* on parole for bank robbery. Or that most buses were as predictable as flash floods or comets. And that some routes reeked of urine. Or that some of the riders were somnambulists numb to their surroundings — government clerks, students, teenage moms, and Marx's lumpenproletariat, that "reserve army of labour," who are surplus to the needs of production at any particular time.

The city's oldest bank robber stared at Harold and muttered, "Fucken rakins."

In hindsight, the raccoons may have been an omen. Three feet tall and plastered to the sides of the bus. One rakin was holding a lobster body; another was carrying a suet bird feeder as if he was a looter. Harold had been terrified of the masked bandits ever since he had been bitten at a cottage.

Perhaps Harold should have known about the rakin bus, but he didn't. Perhaps the transit person should have told him when he inquired about Ride-a-Bus Day, a council initiative to boost ridership that rewarded every rider with a bus-shaped fridge magnet.

When Harold arrived at the depot — the one where knife fights broke out, where drug deals went down as often as the sun — there it was: the No. 99 custom-wrapped as a mobile advertisement for pest control. Somebody's idea of a good idea.

Call Able Pest Control
For Raccoons, Squirrels, Rodents & Birds.
Quick discreet service

The night before Harold had attended a ninety-fifth birthday party at a seniors' home, bringing a card, flowers, and greetings from the mayor.

"How's your father?" someone had asked Harold, as they always did.

"Still causing trouble."

Harold was attractive in a platitudinous way. He had short grey hair and a habit of swinging his arms round and round as though he was warming up for a swim race. There was a hound-dog quality to his long earnest face, and when he smiled, his lower lip rolled under.

"We need more troublemakers in this country."

Harold laughed too enthusiastically. He and his father could not have been less alike. Jock Fox had been a foreign correspondent, an investigative journalist with a satellite phone and a safari jacket. The man who brought someone down somewhere—he could tell you all about it.

•

The first "friend" that Jock Fox brought home was Linda, a producer.

No one caught her last name, but there she was on Christmas Eve 1972 in the Fox living room, embodying the zeitgeist of the seventies in a brown leather skirt and a snug striped sweater. Pierre Trudeau was in power, the sexual revolution was in full swing, and everyone, including

Harold, was expected to offer Linda sweet-and-sour meatballs and a piece of Mom's dark fruitcake.

Linda's relationship with Jock was not spelled out, although it was obvious to Harold, who was then a teen. In subsequent years with subsequent women, the word "friend" was invariably used, as in "your father's friend."

"Are you from here, Linda?" asked Harold, as his mother made eggnog in the kitchen.

"Ah no, Windsor," Linda replied, and for clarification, "Ontario."

"Never been there."

"It's not that nice."

Linda wore her hair long and flat like Michelle from The Mamas and the Papas, and Harold's sister, Joan, the family suck-up, told her, "It looks pretty." Linda acted demure, even though there she was, unexplained, on Christmas Eve, in a bungalow with reindeer snow stencils on the windows and a room-divider draped in garland. And under the tree, a ladies' beret-and-scarf set.

The bus wrap had invisible perforations that allowed passengers to see out, which was, for Harold, a relief. He liked to know where he was going.

Ronnie, the driver, slowed at a stop where a lone woman with grocery bags was waiting, and then, just as she stepped forward, floored it. *Oh dear, look into that,* Harold made a mental note as the woman dropped her bags. *No need for that.*

She has that look, Harold admitted, as the bus rumbled

away, that numb look that told him she had figured it out—the great social conspiracy—the look of people who had realized they would never visit Paris, never enjoy the swim-up bar in Punta Cana, or have health insurance. Never send their children to a private school. And Harold always hoped, he always imagined, that they had a secret pleasure—an illuminated shrine to the Boston Bruins or a grandson who held their hand on walks, blissfully jumping in puddles and calling them, with as much love as you could bear, Nana.

Harold turned his head to catch a final glimpse of the woman, and suddenly he felt dead tired. So tired that he was afraid his eyes would close and he would miss something.

He had a bad sleep again last night. For weeks, he had been having the same dream: he was on Prince Edward Island where they had impossible white beaches, horses tucked in every barn, and Japanese tourists on pilgrimages to the house where an imaginary red-haired girl once slept. After weeks of rain, the sun appeared. It was so brilliant that people didn't know what to do with themselves—it was as though they had walked in on a surprise birthday party. Restaurants set up outdoor tables, streets were closed, and a band was playing elevator music. On one street, a boy with a soother in his mouth was—at the urging of his older sister—dancing. He would stop, and she would wave her arms, and he would dance again. Wildly, out of time with the music.

Five tourists had a stranger take their photos with an iPad—they were wearing turbans: red, gold, and orange.

And then someone said, "Look, there's Harold Fox, the councillor." And there he was: atop a horse like Roy Rogers or Willie Shoemaker, but it wasn't a trick horse or a racehorse. It was a beige miniature pony named Scrub. And people were angry. They were angry at Harold for putting all of his weight on a tiny horse that was supposed to be for children or for pulling a scaled-down wagon in parades.

"What's wrong with him?" someone shouted. "What's wrong with him?"

Harold willed himself awake. Ronnie was riding the bumper of a Fiat 500. Hard. Up so close that you could feel the driver's panic. A diesel-fume-spewing beast bearing down upon her. Harold sighed. *Oh dear.*

Across the aisle two new passengers were seated under an ad for adult literacy. The man was wearing a soft-green sweater with moth holes. A scruff of a beard. On his feet were Blundstones, and on his shaggy head a toque with a tassel, which he kept whipping around, amusing himself, if not the woman.

"He's obsessed with dinosaur porn," the woman said, trying to sound blasé and bacchanalian at the same time. She was wearing a man's tuxedo and holding a red 3 a.m. street-vendor's rose, proof she had been out all night.

"I've heard that."

"E-books mainly. *Taken by a Pterodactyl.*" She seemed unaware of her surroundings.

"Didn't know that."

Harold was tempted to tell the tuxedo woman that he had sat on a committee at the museum when it had that dinosaur exhibit with Sue the T. Rex, the most complete Tyrannosaurus rex skeleton ever found. But then the door opened and Ronnie got into a heated exchange with a woman trying to board with a tray of four Iced Capps. "It's the rules, lady, it's the rules," he said, so she left the drinks on the sidewalk.

When Harold was still a teen, before there were such things as Iced Capps or dinosaur porn, he showed up at a family barbeque in white tennis shorts. At the time, Harold was trying to invent himself as an athlete.

"Oh hi, Harold," someone had said. "Were you at the club?"

"Yes," Harold replied, pleased.

Harold had tried to imagine himself across the net from Borg, or his favourite, Jimmy Connors. He tried to imagine himself delivering a two-handed backhand as though it were nothing, on the grass of Wimbledon with royalty and rock stars in the stands. But when Harold tried to speak to his father, Jock waved him aside impatiently. *Not now!*

Jock was not a handsome man. Part of his appeal was his comical and droopy face that put some in mind of former Quebec premier René Lévesque. Jock was a drinker, a fighter, a carouser. He was one of a succession of journalists to adopt the bemused, befuddled stutter that suggested he was overwhelmed by a cavalcade of emotions, so caught up the magnitude of the event that he could barely speak.

The next morning, Jock left home without a word, overnight bag in hand. And Harold's mother gave her son that look-what-you-have-done-it's-all-your-fault look.

And the door slammed, and after that, Harold remembered to keep his legs covered in the company of his bandy-legged father; he slouched to hide his height; he made a point of never blocking the light of The Great Man.

"A lot of people admire your father," Harold's mother had scolded, as though this had to be said. "An *awful lot* of people."

Harold gave his seat to a young mom with a stroller. He could feel his eyes swelling; he was allergic to dogs, but there were no dogs on the bus, were there? He felt his phone vibrating and he checked Twitter. Harold didn't care for social media, but you couldn't get by without it these days. Some of the councillors were obsessed.

There was also a group of deadbeats who followed council's every breath and tweeted about it. "Howler monkeys," the younger councillors called them." Like Dougal MacDougall, who sat through twelve-hour council sessions and tweeted his bloody heart out, MacDougall who had run against Harold in the last election and placed a sorry fourth, Dougal who planned to run again, ignoring the only thing that mattered in politics: *People have to like you.* People did *not* like Dougal MacDougall, who always looked dirty and had this annoying Scottish accent that sounded like the pads on your brakes had worn down. And he was so *negative. So bloody negative.*

In politics, you tell people what they want to hear—that you knew their grandmother or that they made the best mustard pickles ever—and before long the truth and the non-truths merged like the tracks of a song, and it was a better song, richer and more complete. People liked Harold Fox because he saw the best in others. "Only God can judge," he told a homeless man he got a bed for at a shelter. "Your children have such good manners," he told a single mom who had lost her apartment heat.

Harold looked at his phone and, sure enough, Dougal MacDougall (@VoteDougal) was tweeting: *Is Ride-a-Bus Day the answer? Or improved infrastructure?*

The bus stopped outside a hospital and sleep-deprived shift workers filed on-board. Some attached to headphones, one man wearing a ball cap with a screened photo under Papa's Pride and Joy. Through the window, Harold saw a crossing guard picking up butts and pocketing them.

"Move back," Ronnie shouted to the bus. "Move the hell back."

Harold checked his phone: four missed calls from his lawyer and his wife. Marge was too emotional lately, and it wasn't just her age. Their daughter, Amanda, and her husband, the paramedic, had split up and she seemed intent on transferring her pain.

"He did drugs, you know," Amanda told Marge.

"What kind of drugs?"

"He got Vicodin at work."

"Okay." Marge struggled for words. "It's all for the better then."

"What? That he has ruined my life? *That's* for the better?"

And when Marge tried to explain herself, Amanda lashed out like she did when trapped by her own decisions: "You should talk, with Dad."

Twenty minutes after she had boarded, the Iced Capps woman arrived at her destination and said, "Thank you for a very professional ride," in an extra cheery voice to show that she was over it. And Ronnie replied, "It's a job, lady, it's a job."

The bus was "ahead of schedule," so Ronnie disembarked outside a strip mall. Once outside, Ronnie began talking to a giant, who looked about six-foot-five and three hundred pounds. He was wearing shorts. His bald head was topped by a navy watch cap, rolled up once so that it sat on his huge head like a cherry on a whipped-cream dessert. His upper body was stuffed into a plaid work shirt, and when he moved fully into view — like a container ship turning in the harbour—Harold could see that both calves were covered with tattoos. The giant handed something to Ronnie, who returned to the bus.

Two stops later, a shock of menthol-smelling cologne hit Harold's nostrils. It was emanating from a shady character with a red GoodLife bag, who had assumed the position next to Harold, feet aggressively spread. Hood up. Harold was sure he had seen his face before under the warning: *Do not approach or confront this person.*

Okay, Harold wanted to say, *you're clearly a criminal. And you probably got free bus tickets in that gun-amnesty program I voted against: Turn in your AK-47 and get fifty bus tickets worth one hundred dollars. I knew that was a bad idea.*

The rakin bus was jammed now, jowl to jowl, but Tassel Man and Tuxedo Woman were still debating life. The woman, Harold decided, was a compulsive talker—she probably had a syndrome.

"We don't have much in common," she explained. "He's an anarchist, paintball gun—"

Harold felt like telling her that he had once been shot in the head by a paintball gun at a demonstration, and it was no small matter. And then the woman, who had up to now seemed oblivious of her surroundings, said: "What's wrong with him?"

"Hell if I know," said Tassel Man.

"Well. He's! *Not!* Moving!"

Harold looked at a window seat, and sure enough, a man appeared to be unconscious. He was wearing a scarlet turban.

"Everyone stay in their seats," ordered Ronnie who had pulled the bus over on an overpass with trucks roaring by. "Nobody moves."

"Shit, shit, shit," someone said and then typed on their iPhone.

All around Harold, phones came out, and after a minute, he brought his out too.

No. 99 passengers stranded on Ride-A-Bus Day. Ironic.

Someone tweeted as Harold's eyes began to swell up and close. Benadryl. He needed Benadryl. Harold was wheezing, short of breath.

@Murray

Harold Fox is on the stranded bus. Standing next to me.  *#rakinbus*

@VoteDougal

Are you sure? #rakinbus

Yep. He seems to be having a breathing problem. #rakinbus

Surprised he is there. #rakinbus

Almost everyone—except the bank robber with the Steampunk glasses and the man in the turban—had a device out. The old man looked even more angelic with his eyes closed, Harold thought. *Good Lord, he isn't dead, is he? No. There's a twitch.*

The GoodLife criminal was getting nervous.

Two weeks ago, the police had found a sawed-off shotgun on a bus. It was the night of Harold's thirty-fifth wedding anniversary, and Harold had taken time to call the driver. Harold was—a psychologist might argue—an overcorrector, determined to avoid all of his father's shortcomings. Because his father had travelled throughout Harold's childhood, Harold never left town. Because his father had been a serial philanderer, Harold never looked at another woman. Because his father considered himself a libertarian and a shit disturber, Harold became a Boy Scout leader, as reliable as rhubarb.

Harold believed he had figured it out. Harold believed he had found a path to sanity and sobriety. It was, in hindsight, like that man who decided that he was going to live among the grizzlies in Alaska, and *he did*—naming them, touching them, playing with the cubs—and he talked his girlfriend into joining him in his improbable alternate dimension. And it was all okay until a grizzly ate them. The horrible sounds recorded by the victims' video camera for six long minutes. It was kind of like that.

"You need to see a doctor," Harold's wife had told him. "You need to."

"I will."

"No, you won't. You can't admit that you have a problem."

Harold could barely breathe now. *Did someone smell like dog?*

At the seniors' home, a resident named Mabel had a photo of a beautiful golden Lab on her bedside table. Lucky was his name. Mabel's son had killed someone in a bar fight and was in prison, and he had, until *that* night, been the perfect son. And life looked different after that, Harold decided. After you had opened the newspaper and known *that* person: the teenager who had dropped a boulder off a bridge, killing the minivan driver; the volunteer firefighter charged with arson. You had known them, and they seemed—despite the news—just like You and Me. No better. No worse. They were just *people* who had done something awful that forever defined them. Mabel had touched Harold's arm and said: "You just have to put yourself in God's hands, Harold."

Jock had a list of confidantes he had phoned at 3 a.m. with conspiracies and gossip. And one by one, Jock dropped them, the same people who had appeared on Christmas Eve or at the cottage. This made Harold's sister Joan anxious; she lived in fear of the same cold fate. After years of being the family suck-up, it would be like missing the final payment on a life insurance policy and then dying.

Harold, on the other hand, *knew* Jock would do it. He knew, in the same way that he knew the Leafs would lose in the first round of the playoffs. After years of living in obsequiousness, you would not even know what you had done. It would simply be Jock, The Great Man, showing one last time that he was beholden to no one, and you would, in the words of the Bible, be "shut out from the presence of the Lord and from the glory of his might." *So why would you worry about your father?* Harold asked himself time and time again. *Why would you, at your age, give a damn?*

Ronnie was out of his seat, blocking the door, his creepy-clown tattoo laughing.

When Harold was at the bus terminal, he had spoken to an older man sitting on a bench. The man was clearly lost. And when he looked up at Harold, he told the same story he told six times a day. "I got injured at the dockyard, they gave me opioids. They turned me into a drug addict." The man was trying hard to be forceful, but he had run out of something—outrage, conviction. "A heroin addict, man. A heroin addict."

Harold slipped the man a twenty. The man kept talking, and the more he spoke the more illogical his story became. He told Harold that he was going to be at a hearing next week . . . and he had been the only Black man in the shop . . . and he had been trying to get that hearing for thirty-seven years. "Thirty-seven years, man."

If there was one thing that Harold knew it was this: people's stories often do not add up, and that does not matter.

Harold thought about texting Marge, and then there was a rumble throughout the bus, low and urgent as a train. Harold thought about saying something, but there were moments when Harold—the Voice of Ward 4—was tired of his own voice, and, in those moments, he dreamed of a house in the country near a beach that felt like the afterlife.

The bus door opened and @Murray tweeted.

Shit just got real. #rakinbus

There they were, the men in uniform. The first one had a buzz cut and yellow lettering on his sleeve. The passed-out passenger had come back to life; he may have just fainted.

And then the sheriff said, "You'll have to come with us."

And yes, Harold was supposed to be in court, but the whole matter was a misunderstanding and he'd explained all that. He had not stolen a red cent from the seniors' home and the Boys and Girls Club was getting that TV—it was just taking time. And no, he did *not* have a gambling problem—who didn't enjoy the Casino Caribbean buffet on Wednesdays?—he was just stressed, inordinately incurably stressed, from fixing everyone's problems, from trying to be perfect every single day.

Harold couldn't breathe now.

@Murray

Sheriffs have Harold Fox in custody. 🦝*#rakinbus*

@JoeyMac

Awww shit. I like Harold. He should have run for it.☹️🦝*#rakinbus*

It Will Happen

James d'Entremont had been running for the bus.

The No. 99 had never—in thirty years—arrived at the same time and on this day it was early. James couldn't afford to be late for school, he couldn't afford trouble, so he ran—hoping that the driver with the creepy-clown tattoo would not pull away, pretending, as he often did, not to see him.

It is hard to describe what it feels like to be hit by 3,500 pounds of metal, travelling at fifty kilometres an hour. The bumper of a 1996 Dodge Grand Caravan hit James's right hip, sending him skyward. To James, his spiral through the air felt in slow motion, and he could later recall the vague sensation of one Adidas track shoe flying off.

People turned their heads when it happened because the sound was awful: the sound of fear, the thud of the unforeseeable, a low lament from the pavement. They turned their heads as gawkers do, and they squinted. It was an uncommonly sunny day for Halifax, and the scene seemed overlit as though someone was making a TV movie with Ethan Hawke.

Backlit by the strangeness of what had happened, James took on a surreal form. Motionless, no longer a person, he could have been a struck porcupine or a velour sofa that had toppled off the back of a delivery truck.

James had blond hair, that much you could see from the sidelines. Like many fair young men, he had yet to grow a real beard. If James was on a Florida beach forming a human pyramid, instead of lying broken on a grimy street, he would be in the middle row, but your eyes would be drawn to him because of his sun-streaked hair and his smile. When James's smile escaped, it was as lovely as a chance encounter at the mall with your primary teacher, the nice one who brought a hamster to school and let you name it.

Face down, James had landed in a bed of shattered grille parts, and he thought, for a moment, that he would jump up and walk away before people noticed. He tried to lift his right leg, but it was numb. As James lay on the street, his thinking was so scrambled that he worried about the pink-winged fairy floating before his eyes, all organza and glitter. *Was she cold?*

James was alone on the hot pavement, but extras quickly filled in the scene. In the costumes of college students, store clerks, and bankers. They stood apart from him, as though ordered by a director, and they appeared to go about their imaginary business, as good extras do, while the emergency people arrived.

Gravel was imbedded in James's right cheek, his white earphones torn free. Inside his backpack was a laptop with a download of *Giant Killing*, the Japanese anime story of a struggling soccer team and its coach, the once-great Tatsumi Takeshi. Underneath was a textbook on Carl Jung, one sentence underlined: "In all chaos there is a cosmos, in all disorder a secret order."

*

"I never seen him," a scrawny man told the female cop, who seemed angry, like someone who had once had her heart set on being a large-animal veterinarian and was now doing this. She was wearing aviators, and she seemed angry at everyone, including James.

"I saw him," a senior in wrap-around sunglasses shouted. "I have very good eyesight." Her voice sounded like a shrill phone that would never stop ringing.

"Is he dead?" ventured the scrawny man.

The cop ignored him.

The scrawny man—the one who hit James with his van—was named Bim Shoveller and he belonged to a Facebook group called Cannabis for the Cure. Bim had an open growler on the back seat of his blue Grand Caravan. His anxiety felt like spiders crawling up his leg.

He sat slumped on the curb, head in hands.

Illuminated by the important role of villain, Bim became larger than he was. Part of something grandly ghoulish. Stare-worthy.

Bim had never in his life weighed more than one-hundred-and-forty pounds. He'd been a scrawny kid and a scrawny adult, and sometimes he piled on a gold chain and bracelet for heft. Bim was wearing a white tracksuit that overwhelmed him and made his scrawny neck look scrawnier. He'd kept his hair buzzed ever since one night, while drinking, he let a woman he may have known shave it into a Mohawk.

He pulled out a smoke.

Neither James nor Bim lived anywhere near this street, where tourists roamed in summer and pub crawls formed at night. James was a day student who dutifully took a series of buses across the bridge from Dartmouth, the City of Lakes, while Bim lived in Spryfield, home of the "Real-Life Trailer Park Boys."

The night before, the street had been awash in princesses and paladins, all bidding farewell to Hal-Con, an unrepentant celebration of all things weird: sci-fi, fantasy, gaming, cyberpunk, Steampunk, renaissance, anime. Hal-Con was an unapologetic act of rebellion, the ordinary daring to expose their secrets, donning suits of armour or wired wings. Spinach-green face paint. It was an opera of escapism in a city that had once been blown to bits, a city that had solemnly buried *Titanic* victims, adorning the coffins of the unknown with bouquets of lilies.

When James d'Entremont was still on the pavement, he looked up at the paramedic, a big capable man in Ray-Bans, the kind of man who built his own fishing camp in the woods. Who cleared his neighbour's driveway in winter. *Will he make the phone call?* he wondered. *To my mother? I hope it is him.*

James was worried about his mother, worried about overloading her circuit of pain, his mother, who had become one of those people whose heart explodes when a phone rings or a knock comes at the door. Have you seen them: the ghost parents? The ones who walk for miles and miles alone. Or slide into Starbucks with the one friend they can talk to. And their eyes are in the distance on something you cannot see, and there is no joy in their being. It has been drained from their electro-shocked bodies. Their life is illuminated by one dingy ceiling fixture—the round one that fills with dust and dead insects, so dim that they can barely distinguish colours—and everyone else's life is lit by pot lights.

James saw, before he lost consciousness, a homeless man with a shopping cart. A cyclist. He saw the female cop in aviators writing in her notebook, and he wondered if she was a real cop or a Hal-Con cosplayer who had escaped into fantasy. *Katie Fallis, 22, describes herself as a struggling art student, and spent four months sewing her cosplay costume of Undyne the Undying for Undertale.*

He tried to smile but he couldn't.

James d'Entremont was good at two things in life: soccer, which had consumed him since the age of four, and sketching. He had an aptitude for faces, and he drew comic strips, including one of a boy named Havoc, who turned up at crime scenes and located missing persons. James sometimes showed his comics to Dennis, his friend since the age of six, Dennis who had started to wear a rainbow headscarf, as though he was Dennis Hopper deep in the jungle of *Apocalypse Now*. His thing, he would tell you, was "karma."

The last conversation James had before he was hit by the van was with his friend Dennis:

"I'd like to invent a phone with a built-in code of conduct," Dennis had announced. "Call someone for no good reason and you get a mild shock. Do it again, you get a stronger shock. Keep phoning every five minutes —because you suspect they are there and just not answering—you get a shock that knocks you out cold."

"Cool."

"Leave a non-message: 'Ohhhhhhhhh, Dennis, I guess you aren't answering your phone,' you get put in a semi-permanent coma."

"Could a phone do that?"

"I was speaking as a philosopher—"

"So basically, you wanna put your mother in a coma?"

"Yes."

"Is that good karma?"

"Point, dude, point."

•

Bim Shoveller was good at two things in life: playing pool and making large trays of lasagna. He had been thinking about hamburger lasagna when he went to his mother's house in Spryfield that day, a scrubby prefab with fluorescent plastic flowers stuck in a chain-link fence. Neon pink roses and purple carnations that would never be found in nature.

When Bim walked through the front door, he could smell fried clams from a takeout, and that meant that Bradley was having his favourite meal. Bradley, the baby, his mother's pet.

His mother, Lela, was wearing a furry turquoise housecoat, and she clutched the front with one hand in a defensive manoeuvre when she saw Bim. Lela was short with a brittle perm. Her face was always in the crouch position, as though her tight mouth and eyes could come at you at any time.

The last conversation Bim had before he hit James was with his mother, Lela:

"Where's Bradley?" Bim asked as the sun poured in a window, illuminating particles of dust, as well as the absence of Bradley, the pet.

"He just gone out."

"Okay."

"Didn't ya hear?"

"Hear what?"

"They took away some of his money —!"

Bim shook his shaved head, as though he was knocking all the cogs into place.

"How did you *not* hear that?" she demanded, as though Bim should be on top of everything involving Bradley, who never remembered anyone's birthday or knew how many cousins he had, Bradley who was on a disability pension for tinnitus. Lela's eyes took a jab at his head: "He never got a call or nothin'."

"That sounds weird."

"WEIRD? Is that what you be calling it?"

Bim let out his own sigh, one of those I-don't-need-any-more-shit sighs. "What does he say?"

"He says it's because he told one of them bastards to go fuck herself. That's what they do; they get you, them bastards."

"Leave it to Big Mouth Bradley."

"Why would you say that about Bradley?" And the look she gave Bim was so mean, so hateful, that he felt ashamed for living, he felt ashamed for everything he had done in his forty-eight years on this Earth. "You rotten no-good bastard." And then as Bim headed for the door and the beer store, she shouted: "Didya leave me that money I need? Didya?"

•

James's mother raced to the hospital when she got the call. Her son was in a room with a ninety-year-old woman with kidney failure and dementia, a curtain pulled so that he could not witness her slow, inevitable death. Overtaken by panic, his mother momentarily mistook the near-dead body for her son.

She was still shaken when she stood next to James's bed.

"Why?" she sobbed.

"It'll be okay," James told her. "It'll be okay." And then, as he always did, he sighed, "This is nothing, Mom. *Right?* This is nothing."

Sometimes, life is that hitchhiker you pick up on a lonely stretch of highway. You drive through the night, sharing coffee and stories, until you leave him at an Irving truck stop and discover — at a stark tollbooth on the

Cobequid Pass manned by a woman old enough to be your mom—that he stole your wallet. Life can be as cruel as Ming the Merciless.

And here is what you may wonder: what does it take to push someone to the precipice, to the point where they lose faith in God and themselves, when the weight of family and fate becomes too much? It depends, doesn't it, on how many blows they have already taken. A family that loses a child is never the same; you can't wish it different. That's how it was for James and his mother after Martin died. Those families—all of them—were like people who were on a boat that exploded, and they were now in the black, bottomless ocean trying to stay afloat. It was terrifying because they didn't know where land was, they didn't know what was beneath them. Every now and then they lost sight of each other, and the grief hit them like a mouthful of brackish water, and they panicked. Sometimes they thought about letting it take them. If you were in the water, it was your job to resist. It was your job to let your mother think that you were safe, and just because Martin was gone, in a tragedy too awful to be real, you were both going to make it.

After Bim was interviewed by the angry cop, he drove home and fired up a spliff. He lived above George's Pizza Donairs & Subs: Spryfield's Premier Pizzeria, which sold a sixteen-inch donair pizza for sixteen dollars. Two blocks from his mother's house, he felt safe there. Bim turned on his surveillance camera, which gave him a clean view of his steps. He put on Wu-Tang Clan.

Some say karma isn't real—it is a concept created to keep people in their place, from seeking retribution. A panacea. It tells them that bad things will happen to bad people, when, in fact, they rarely do. Bad things happen to good families like the d'Entremonts whose teenage son died of cancer. In a hospital bed surrounded by loved ones who kept talking to the very end because there was a chance he might hear them saying "I love you" over and over again.

Life does, however, sometimes accidentally correct itself.

Bim Shoveller had a Glock 19 semi-automatic in the dash of his Grand Caravan that day, and he was going to use it. Bim, who had been in prison for eight and a half years for assault with a deadly weapon, assault causing bodily harm, and the full set of drug charges. If James had not run in front of him, Bim would have kept driving to Rite Clean Dry Cleaners across the Angus L. Macdonald Bridge, and he would have shot a man named Cyril Rafuse with the bestselling pistol in the USA. He would have to tell you why.

The angry cop could have opened Bim's dash and found the loaded Glock, but she didn't. Instead she issued a ticket to James d'Entremont.

A 19-year-old pedestrian was struck by a motor vehicle at the corner of Barrington and Spring Garden at 2:20 p.m. He has been taken to hospital with injuries. He was charged under a section of the Motor Vehicles Act, which is a pedestrian *moving into the path of a vehicle when impractical for a vehicle to stop. It carries a fine of $512.*

Bim closed his eyes and let the dope settle in his lungs. He stared at one hand where he had three words tattooed in Gothic font: Eat Sleep Glock.

James d'Entremont missed a full season of soccer. He spent three days in hospital with the old lady, who died in her sleep, and one week later he went to school on crutches. His mother drove him. James met the love of his life in a psych class of five hundred students when she held the door open for him. She was a small girl with black hair and eyes as blue as delphiniums. It was, as the cliché goes, as though he had known her all of his life. And she was both different from him and the same.

Bim Shoveller was shot outside a donair shop on Canada Day 2017, and his mother told a TV reporter, "He had a heart of gold."

In three years' time, James d'Entremont and Margaret O'Flaherty will move to Ireland where her parents live next to a brook inhabited by fairies. The young fairies have clear gossamer wings, and the older ones have wings of diverse colours, dark yellow for the most important. They have underground tunnels and special trees where they meet. And people leave them gifts: beads, flower petals, coins, and glitter. And for James, it will be as though he had stood at the edge of a pond and taken a running leap and jumped from rock to rock to rock, and when he made it across, his past was on the other side, and all that was ahead of him was newness.

James will go on to write and illustrate graphic novels, and he will have the loveliest children you have ever seen, and just like Martin, the little boy will be thoughtful — so thoughtful that he will cover the family cat with a blanket when it goes to sleep, he will pick his mother daisies. James's mother will come to live with them, and her grandchildren will make her as happy as she can be, and her muted happiness will smell like a fistful of wildflowers.

And all of that will happen, because it has to.

Dirty Little Lair

With David, it was all over in under a minute.

Usually, when you show up for a job interview and the fix is in, the reality dawns on you slowly. The person conducting the interview is distracted, the handshake feels tepid. The chair they give you is wobbly. Or in the burning sun. Maybe you notice that someone else is sitting outside, someone's perfidious nephew.

With David, the jig was up before he could remove his tan topcoat. It was like being carjacked on a Sunday morning at a stoplight on your way to a pancake breakfast.

"Well," the HR woman announced without to-do, "we filled the job this morning."

"Ahh," muttered David.

The HR woman wore a queer look, like she was trying to feign pity or confusion, like she wasn't the person who had phoned David and asked him to come in, as though he had just wandered in off the street in a lavender cape and crown.

"But we'd like to know why you were interested in—*ahem*—us."

And this is what should have happened:

"Because I am an idiot?" David should have replied. "Because all of the astronaut positions were filled. Because I am a desperate man willing to sell my soul to the lowest bidder. Because I just elected to sit next to a madman on a bus when other seats were available."

"Ahhh. And what is it about the newspaper's Custom Content Department that interests you?"

"What a silly question," David should have chuckled. "Look at your walls, look at those mounted layouts from your auto supplement: *Epic Day on the Range. Chasing powder and thrills on four wheels*, and the one on home renovations: *Every Cook's Dream Kitchen*. Look at the garish photos and florid headlines pointing readers to the nearest retail outlet.

"To me, Custom Content is the Wal-Mart of news, serving shoddy goods to the underclass. And in the same way that Wal-Mart jeans look like *real* jeans to the people who drive into the city on Saturday in a rusty Cobalt, Custom Content stories look like real stories. With bylines and photos. They are ubiquitous. And everyone can understand them because they are written for that apocryphal reader, the one with the grade 9 education.

"And I like that, I guess."

What really happened:

David's body went into fight-or-flight mode; his lungs took in extra air. David, sitting there in his sincere haircut, and who had spent forty minutes on the bus and then circled on foot so as not to be early. And so, he sputtered out answers he could not later recall, answers about putting his experience to good use and moving with the times, his voice cracking like an old phonograph recording.

"Thank you," the HR woman said coldly. "Maybe next time."

David's mother had become — in her old age — obsessed with people sleeping. It was, she believed, a sign of weakness, mental illness, or sloth, and, driven by this distorted thinking, she took it upon herself to catch people in bed. Muriel would ring David's doorbell at 8 a.m. on a Sunday, and when his wife, Susie, raced to the door in her housecoat, there would be Muriel, holding a bottle of jam.

"You weren't in bed, were you?" Accusatory.

"Ahhh, nooo," Susie would lie.

"I just came from the market." Proud. "And I got you this jam."

Then, gone. In her car, careening around corners.

David's mother could not remember that people had predicaments that had nothing to do with her. She could not accept the fact that David, who was attempting to freelance after his twenty-year newspaper job had been axed, was often writing, and had convinced herself that he was instead sleeping.

That night — at 10 p.m. — she phoned.

"Were you in bed?"

"Yes." Too weak to lie.

"WHAT? This early?"

"I had a meeting this morning." Why was he answering this absurd question knowing that it would lead to an absurd response?

"Well, I have been up since 3 a.m.!"

"Okay."

*

That morning, when the sun was still bright and optimistic, David had asked Susie, "Do I look too old in this jacket?"

"No."

"I think it will go well."

"They'll be lucky to get you."

When David met Susie, she was tall with straight brown hair and the face of a greyhound. Curious eyes, a long nose, and a minor mouth. Her bangs covered her eyebrows and her hair concealed the outer regions of her cheeks. It was as though someone had put an armoured hood on a greyhound's delicate head and now it was protected.

"Is the red tie too aggressive?" he asked.

"Maybe the blue . . ."

Her hair was now flecked with grey, but her head was still, David would tell you, as delicate as hope.

*

David could have taken any seat on the bus, but instead, he took *that* one. *Why?* he later asked himself. To prove that he was open-minded? Good with strangers? In any event, the man started in at once.

"You can look up anything online, ya know."

"Sure," agreed David.

"Where your ex lives. How much a Russian bear dog costs."

"Yep."

"They'll run ya about thirteen hundred US. I'd love to have one, a black one. Have you ever seen the size of their heads? Maybe when I get my own place—"

"That would be nice."

"Didya know"—his voice rising to an uncomfortable level—"that they are extremely, *extremely* proud. They will *never ever* back down in a fight. One guy had one, and it took down seven grey wolves. Didya know that?"

"Well no, I didn't," said David.

"Well then, you don't know fuck."

•

"Oh dear," Susie sighed when David arrived home that day.

It was my fault, David thought about saying, but then he changed his mind. It wasn't. They had clearly advertised for an editor, not a messenger, a galley slave, or a serf. Not a rodeo clown or a male prostitute. And he was an editor, wasn't he, someone who had worked on the national desk for ten years. And why did they drag him in there if there was no job? To see if he was wearing a fedora?

"I should have stood up and left their dirty little lair," David said.

And Susie sighed again, "Oh dear."

On his way to Custom Content, David had passed the real newsroom, much like the one where he had spent his career, a room that had obsessed him and owned him, rewarded him and betrayed him. He could feel the rhythm and the sounds. He had kept going to Custom Content, and when he arrived, he felt like someone ducking into a payday loan company, afraid to be seen. But he didn't tell Susie that.

"The whole farce lasted a good twenty minutes. After they told me the job was filled, the first idiot brought in a second idiot, a poseur with a man bun, and he pretended to take notes on me."

"Maybe," his wife suggested improbably, "they wanted to see what a real newsman looked like."

"Maybe."

Each morning, David took a walk along the river, where he could sometimes spot a bald eagle or a muskrat. He often encountered a white-haired man with a bicycle. The man had a frying pan and a sleeping bag, and he was homeless. The man collected pop cans, and one day, when David tried to strike up a conversation, the man harrumphed: "I was at sixty-one," his can count interrupted. After that, David let him be.

Another morning, the man approached David, upset and rambling. Someone, a walker, had said something to him. "Yes, I sleep in there when it is raining." The man pointed to a public washroom — a cement enclosure — along the trail. "But I always leave it clean and I don't bother no one, and *yes*, I am homeless."

The man's white hair was long, his clothes were frayed,

and at that moment, the sight of him made David cry. The *poète maudit* eyes, the once-handsome face, the way that life had taken sides against him. People can die, you know, of broken-heart syndrome; it's a real thing named takotsubo cardiomyopathy. After a terrible event, part of the heart becomes enlarged and does not pump the way it is supposed to, and this can be fatal.

David stepped forward and shook the man's hand. "Just live your life." And if David had been writing a feature story about the kindness of strangers, the man would have taken comfort in the gesture, and the scene would have wrapped itself up in a bright red bow.

But it wasn't a story; it was life. And so, the man seemed annoyed by the handshake; he just wanted to tell David, "They can all go straight to hell."

And here is what should have happened that day:

When David boarded the bus on his way to the newspaper, he would *not* have taken a seat next to the madman with button pins on his jacket: *Vote Trump for President. Learn from Wild Animals. Be Kind to Me, I Have Rosacea.*

He would have sat across from a rangy girl with her hair in a braid. And she would have been wearing, instead of pins, a gold heart-shaped locket, and it would have contained two besotted souls, facing each other and all of life's struggles. The old-fashioned locket would have been deep enough to hold a perfect love story. Hers or his and Susie's. Their meeting in a bookstore. Their very first date.

The months she had stayed by his side when his world turned upside down and he almost fell off.

There was a time when every little girl wanted a heart-shaped locket, and the Christmas catalogue was filled with silver ones on flimsy chains. They didn't open, but they were pretty, and they put a smile on someone's face, and a little girl felt loved, and wasn't that all anyone wanted?

And David would have gotten off at the very next stop. He would have walked back home. And Susie would not have been wearing a housecoat when he arrived; Susie would not be dying.

They would have talked about buying that old house on the Eastern Shore and opening a craft brewery. They would have talked about getting a boat and having a picnic on an island. And then they would have put on their jackets and gone for a walk, down along the river, and maybe they would have seen the old man, and he would have been happily counting his cans.

Would You Recommend Us?

The Halifax Bulletin

Your news lifeline to Nova Scotia and the world for 87 years.

Exit Interview

*Your opinion is important to us. Your responses are strictly confidential and will only be used for statistical purposes (**except in the event we are legally required to disclose information**).*

Name: Harry Egan
Department: Newsroom
Hire Date: Feb. 1, 1984

Supervisor: John Stringer
Position: Night Editor
End Date: Dec. 24, 2017

Reason for Departure:

☐ Relocation/Move
☐ End of Contract
☐ Work Environment
☐ Direct Supervisor
☐ Job Security
☐ Salary
☐ Retirement
☐ Return to School
☑ Other *(specify below)*

Fired without warning.

Have you accepted other employment?

☐ Yes ☑ No

Ahh, I wish.

Would you recommend us to friends and family as a good place to work?

☑ Yes ☐ No

Let me start by saying: It was so very kind of you to send me this survey. Not once, but twice, just days after I was kicked to the curb like a bedbug-infested futon. So very *very* kind. But then again, I would expect nothing less of the HR Department, which has always been top shelf, a paragon of efficiency. I can still hear Krystal Hogg, who reminds me of that affable comedienne Roseanne Barr, ordering me to turn in my employee pass: *"NOW!"* as I was escorted out of the building by an armed security guard named Gino. Out the door I was, ten minutes after I received my layoff notice. Left standing on the sidewalk, holding that clichéd box of belongings—my favourite mug, a thesaurus, and my 25-year service certificate—waiting for someone to retrieve me as though I was a sex-offender released from Archambault, blinking back daylight. Ahh, yes, Krystal, a treasure who graced the newsroom with her presence every month. Krystal, the first to shout "Darwin" every time some poor family in the news lost a son in a tragedy—blown up by fireworks or impaled on a fence. Because not everyone knows that word, Darwin. But *she* does.

But back to the question: *Would I recommend The Bulletin as a good place to work?*

Yes, unambiguously, yes, if you have exhausted all other forms of self-torment: hair-plucking, putting your balls in a metal vice, sitting through an entire season of *Little Mosque on the Prairie*. Then, yes.

PS: I apologize for the six-month delay in returning this survey; I have been occupied.

Please rate the following statements related to the organization as a whole:

1 = Strongly Agree
2 = Somewhat Agree
3 = Somewhat Disagree
4 = Strongly Disagree

Growth and advancement opportunities are available
1 ☐ 2 ☐ 3 ☐ 4 ☑

Employees are treated fairly
1 ☐ 2 ☐ 3 ☐ 4 ☑

The company supports work-life balance
1 ☐ 2 ☐ 3 ☐ 4 ☑

Appropriate administrative policies are in place
1 ☐ 2 ☐ 3 ☐ 4 ☑

Senior management communicates with staff
1 ☐ 2 ☐ 3 ☐ 4 ☑

Overall, how was your experience working here?
Fair. I was on the night shift for 25 of my 30 some years. I wrote some good stories, I edited some bad ones. I can proudly say I removed the word "gobsmacked" from the same reporter's column 15 times. Being on nights did mean

that I gave up all semblance of a personal life; I missed anniversary dinners, birthday parties, and kids' hockey games. But then again, we thought we were doing something important, something that mattered. We thought we were truth brokers and storytellers. We confused the significance of the story we were covering with our own significance, but that is an occupational hazard. The bigger the story, the bigger our buzz. And then came Google and citizen bloggers who eroded the craft, which then defaulted to clickbait, Storify, and Instagram. I suppose that there were times when I was happy, in the same way that people on a sunny beach are happy before a tsunami strikes. But is happiness the primary goal in life? Mindless hedonistic happiness? I don't know.

What did you like best about working here?
The remarkable office ergonomics. (Thanks again to the incomparable HR department which moved us to a "rationalized" workspace two years ago.) In the new *Bulletin* newsroom, one cannot remove a potato chip from a cellophane bag without that noise reaching the ears of others. One cannot clip a fingernail. One certainly cannot have three TVs and two police scanners blaring at all times without going mad. But there is always a silver lining, isn't there? The things I learned about my co-workers thanks to these incredible acoustics. Night after night, I was privy to the most intimate details of personal phone conversations, including George's haranguing of the contractor working on his basement, and Margaret's negotiations with her daughter's volleyball coach. I heard

Fred supervising—from his desk—his two small children; one night he threatened them so loudly, so violently, that I almost called Protective Services, but the children were, in Fred's defence, setting fire to a cat. And Dicky Doiron's monologues, priceless material that you could not even purchase. Night after night. About politics. Sports. Himself. You cannot put a price on that.

What did you like least about working here?

I least liked having met some wonderful characters and then having to leave them behind. Like my union rep, Dougal MacDougall, who lives in my neighbourhood and did absolutely nothing for me when I went on the chopping block. You do not meet men like that every day.

Running into Dougal in the produce section of the grocery just as you were contemplating a box of red lush berries—berries you could dip in chocolate or smother in cream—was like having your new Subaru rear-ended at a crosswalk. Dougal was an original. Who else would roast an entire pig—head intact—on his front lawn on Canada Day, horrifying small children? Or wear a see-through white Speedo to a Polar Bear Dip? Or say things like: "Ima meeting my auld da for brekkie. Ima hoping the eggs benny will be delish." Dougal remained an original. If Dougal had wanted to be less original, he could have bathed. He could have stopped running a condominium for rats in his backyard under the guise of a compost heap. But he didn't. And while he did absolutely nothing for me when I was fired without cause after 30 some years—"downsizing" they called it—he was a character I will never forget.

What suggestions for improvement do you have for us?

I would recommend that you stop outsourcing copy-editing and page design to Third World countries; I would recommend that you stop running advertorials and iPhone photos; I would recommend that you stop lowering the quality of your paper until there is nothing left. But what do I know? I was on the slippery slope for 10 years, and I could not save myself, let alone the business. I am a sad fool who gave up my family for a cardboard box of press passes, earplugs, and a ceramic mug commemorating the marriage of Will and Kate.

If we implemented these suggestions, would you return to work for us?

I would give it thought. I am alone now, living on Eel Island, about 150 kilometres from the city, where I have limited internet but access to the ocean and a boat. Nobody knows what I once did for a living, and if they did, they would not care. I am, I suppose, an anachronism like the ice man or the coal-delivery truck. Ever since I was a child, I have been fascinated by the very big and the very small, so I am researching the life of Anna Swan, Nova Scotia's tragic giantess who stood seven feet, eleven inches and toured with P.T. Barnum. She married another giant—a dandy from Kentucky—with Tom Thumb in attendance, and I am discovering curious facts about the extraordinary house they built in Ohio. The diamonds. The python. Etc. etc. It is all coming together, especially the python angle, and some things have stopped. The tremors. The rage.

The crying. The stalking of *Bulletin* bosses, all of which proved pointless and did result in an unfounded charge of cyberbullying and the suspension of my Facebook account. All of that has stopped. God willing, the drinking is next.

Additional comments and suggestions are welcome.
No, thank you. I am very tired now. I think I will have a nap.

Thank you for taking the time to complete this questionnaire.
Please return it to the Human Resources Department.

Remember

It was hard to miss, a mahogany casket with two portraits on top: one of Mister Logan in his trademark aviators, another of him in stage makeup as Ko-Ko, the Lord High Executioner of Titipu. The casket was draped with an all-white spray of roses, carnations, irises, and freesias. Three white candles to one side.

The casket was in the centre circle of the gym floor where the tip-offs take place. A twelve-foot sphere outlined in blue tape. In an echo chamber two stories high.

A middle-aged couple had made their way to the flower-draped casket.

"He looks so young in that photo," said the woman.

"He loved his operettas, didn't he?" noted the man. "Pink Floyd used a phrase from *The Mikado* in one of their songs: 'a short, sharp shock.' I remember hearing about that years later and thinking, *Mister Logan*."

"I thought about auditioning one year—"

"Did you?"

"No. I did chess club instead. It was only once a week."

They nodded gravely, their duty done.

The high school gym was so big, so expansive, that it was easy to miss things, things right under your nose.

Former students milled about, drinking coffee and eating Costco beet chips. Some, like the couple, marched straight up to the casket; others approached it tentatively, the way one might approach a mysterious sinkhole, afraid they could be swallowed.

Mister Logan—did anyone even know his first name?—had taught English and drama for thirty-five years and he was one of *those* teachers. His father had been a judge, which counted for something back then. He had a master's degree, which also counted for something. But it was his "passion" for his job that distinguished him—he dressed in stage costumes, he held an all-night readathon, he invited students to his lake cottage, and when he retired, the school named the new library for him.

"Too young," people muttered by rote. "Too young."

Outside the trees were full of leaves again and, after a hard winter, the air smelled of blossoms and relief. It was the kind of day that reminded you of yearbooks and summer plans. Freedom.

"Remember when that guy cut off his finger in shop?" asked Steve. "Man, that was gross."

Steve and Les were reminiscing on the sidelines, a solid three-point shot from their dead teacher. Steve was a tall man who looked like he was too busy or too nervous to eat. Len was sturdier. Over the years, his body had thickened and his eyes had narrowed. It was easier to see things that way, things someone else might miss. He had a moustache and his hair was parted, old-school, to one side.

"Kevin, wasn't it?"

"Yeah. His mother had a fit because she had him in

piano. She said: 'There goes his dream!' He hated piano, but she said it was his dream."

They laughed and then stared across the gym, which had a mound of blue nylon crash mats stacked up against one wall; they stared as though they expected Kevin to materialize along with his mutilated hand, a ghoulish memento of their youth.

Outside, a worker was breaking up a concrete step with a pneumatic drill. It sounded like the world's largest dental drill—a frightful whirring noise that turned sharp in places and then went *rat a tat tat. Whirrrrrr whirrrr whirrrr rat a tat tat* right to your nerve endings. Inside, everyone was trying to ignore it.

Some grads were using the occasion as a rehearsal for an upcoming reunion. Others were there to openly gloat. One forgettable classmate had become an orthodontist, and now he had a young wife and the smug look of a man who had his house custom built and posed for the builder's website: "Drew has a personal gym with a 4K TV while Diane has a yoga studio." *Good for you, Drew, good for you*, Steve thought. *Nobody remembers you from high school, so good for you.*

A politician and a school board official had found the sweet spot where everyone could see them and they stood there, expectant. There was hardly any Logan family present, save for a pair of elderly cousins in belted dresses, and they kept asking people, "Who are you?"

"Surprised so many showed up," said Steve.

"Never married; school was his whole thing." Les used his flat cop voice, the one that delineated life into rights and wrongs, innocent and guilty. "You know—" and then it started up again, *whirrrrrr whirrrr whirrrr rat a tat tat.*

This was the same gym where Steve had once shot hoops. Where girls had hung over the balcony to watch. Girls with ironed hair and unbroken hearts. Midi coats. Like Trudy, the prettiest girl in the school. Steve had seen her last week; she was the cosmetics woman at his drugstore, a sketchy operation with shoplifters, Mexican security guards, and methadone scripts. An aging blonde who wore a crisp white smock and valiantly tried to project a professional air, as though she could transform your sorry life through a palette of nude shades. There was something noble about that, Steve had decided, the way she carried on, smiling over the human rubble, as though she never forgot she was *that* girl.

A chattering pest was suddenly in Steve's face.

Oh hi, Steve said, It's Ralph, right? No? Ralph is your brother? Right, right, right. So Ralph had the Triumph motorcycle not you? So you say he's dead and you're Dougie. Sorry to hear about Ralph. Yes, it is tragic about Mister Logan.

And then, as suddenly as he had appeared, Dougie departed, dragging one leg across the hardwood floor, which had, for the occasion, been swept. Steve looked at the gym entrance—the school janitor, a Slavic-looking man well past the age of retirement, had appeared with his push broom, and he stood there for a good long minute, as though he expected everyone to leave; he stood there in his green work shirt and pants, as though this was not right.

When Steve had awoken that morning, an orange poppy had burst open in his yard like a beach umbrella and he took that as a sign. The night before he had made a list of five things he was grateful for and he had carried that list to this place, where everyone was suspended between reality and nostalgia, hard truths and Polaroid memories.

"Remember that fitness test in Centennial year?" he asked Les. "One boy had a hole in his heart, and they still made him do it. He fell down on the long run and started to cry. They yelled 'Get up!' and he said that he couldn't or he might die."

"Brutal."

"Standing long jump."

"A very precise measurement of human beings."

"And sit-ups."

"Another excellent measurement."

"When it was all over, some douche in Ottawa tallied up the results and mailed out certificates. Our school got a bronze and the principal said it was because of the boy with the bad heart: 'If it had not been for Harvey...'"

They laughed, and Steve shuffled the business cards in his pocket. He leaned into the room; he let it absorb him. It felt good, this mindless appearance, this banal chatter that came nowhere near his centre, nowhere near his truth. In the back of the room, where light from a high window hit, under the word *PANTHERS*, was Trudy from the drugstore, and she was smiling and laughing like she was still the prettiest girl in school.

Dougie was back because he couldn't help himself.

No, you aren't a bother, Dougie. Yes, as a matter of fact, I am selling real estate. Why? Are you in the market? Ahhh, that's too bad. Yes, arsenic in the water is very bad. A stroke? Wow. Hope it works out for you.

And then Dougie asked before he limped away again, exaggerating the impediment to make sure his old classmates noticed, "You still a cop, Les?"

"Yep, Dougie. Nothing else I can do."

"I remember the time you wore a diaper in the Twerp Week assembly. Ha ha."

"That was me."

"You were undercover for a while, weren't you?"

"Nah, Dougie. I'm in community outreach. Stopping crime before it starts, giving little kids chocolate milk—"

"All right. I had a stroke, you know. Arsenic."

"We're all just trying to survive, Dougie."

Steve thought about early-morning dances during Twerp Week, pancake breakfasts, and the Miss PHS pageant, held on the same stage as Mister Logan's interminable production of *The Mikado.* He thought about making the A basketball team, along with Les and Bugsy Schmidt, who scored a heroic three-pointer at provincials, Bugsy who had joined the Hells Angels and was now on Interpol's most-wanted list for racketeering and murder. How the hell did that happen? In this town? It wasn't *that* kind of town. It was an innocuous town, a soft town, not the kind of town you could count on in a street fight. A town of busybodies who did "good deeds" and then posted photos of their good deeds online, throwing parties to celebrate their benevolence to strangers.

It was a town that also made up its mind about people and there was nothing you could do about that, Steve decided. Who mattered, who didn't. It was like Steve Fonyo running coast to coast on one leg—covering 7,924 kilometres—after cancer claimed the country's hero Terry Fox; it was like the toothless Leon Spinks beating Muhammad Ali in the ring because he could not, *would not*, tire in fifteen brutal rounds, and people pretending that it never happened. There are underdogs, it seems, and then there are people whom society decides have no business reaching for greatness, no business upsetting the natural order of things.

•

Steve went to the washroom and stood in front of the mirror. Under the fluorescent lights, his skin was sallow, his eyes as tired as his striped cotton shirt. He had lost twenty pounds since chemo. *Think positive thoughts*, he told himself, *use words like* love *and* humanity *and do not forget the blessings in your life.* And then he heard an awkward, "Hallo."

At the next sink was a man who reminded Steve of his former brother-in-law, but it wasn't him because he had moved to Fort Mac and died of cancer. Cancer isn't fun but it happens. And it's not because you ate fried pepperoni or drank beer—it just happens. And you do your best: you watch funny cat videos, you start a new job, you stop reading the daily news orgy of human failings, and you do *not* put a clean biopsy report first on your list of five things to be grateful for because that could jinx it. You make it number three behind a new career in real estate and a cat named Mouse.

The man was having trouble figuring out the faucet, one of those contraptions triggered by a hand movement. "I'm half blind," he blurted.

"Were you always half blind?"

"Yes."

"Okay." Steve felt guilty for asking.

And then Steve looked at the hand that was extended under the baffling faucet, and he saw the missing finger.

Steve was about to tell Les about Kevin—*he is here and he is blind and he's always been blind and they put him in a room with band saws*—when it started. The lights went dim and everyone turned to face one direction. It was a slide show, the title page introducing the Fallen Panthers.

"Oh, man," groaned Steve. "Whose idea was this?"

Les squinted and said nothing.

Mister Logan was in the opening frame—a place of honour, it seemed—followed by a former student who ended up driving a taxi for twenty-five years and then got stabbed.

"Christ! Didn't know Chuck Adams was dead."

"Suicide."

"Man, could he play guitar. He was the only guy I knew who could really play. Some of us had guitars and pretended we could play, but he could. One time, he did 'Stairway to Heaven,' and it was ridiculous."

"Yep."

The parade of the dead continued.

"Donna Murray? She was a sweetheart."

"Yep. MS."

"Look, there's Dougie's brother Ralph. I remember him now."

"Diabetes."

"Remember when Ralph came to school in a cape when he was on acid and the principal asked if he was Batman?"

"Ralph was always stoned."

They both laughed.

whirrrrrr whirrrr whirrrr rat a tat tat

The drill had grown louder, and the janitor was back in the doorway, looking like he needed to say something. What? He had a brush cut, coarse skin, and blunt unpolished features. Steve watched someone scoot across the room to shoo him, but before they arrived, he made a rude hand gesture and left.

*

The slide show ended.

Another old face, this one alive, was in front of Steve.

No, Stretch, my wife isn't here. No, she won't be at the reunion. Well, I am divorced, actually. Oh. Okay. Well that's too bad about your mother. I am sure that nobody blames you. Ah, no. I had no idea you slept with my sister. Imagine that. Ha ha.

Steve was getting tired—the idea had been to come here and "network," to let people know he was in real estate and drum up business. But now he was tired. He was as tired as the brown loafers he had polished to come here.

whirrrrrr whirrrr whirrrr rat a tat tat

And then a podgy man with white hair shuffled by, a man he had known in high school as a drama-club nerd and Bugsy's younger, malleable brother. He had played Pooh-Bah, Lord High Everything Else. The family had lived two streets over from Steve; the dad worked at the shipyard and the mom was a Dominion store cashier.

His name was Nick. And he was wearing shorts and a blue bowling shirt that covered his gut like a tarp. His face was slack as though he did not have the energy to control it, as though he had seen a ghost and it was chasing him around every corner. There was no warmth to his eyes, no depth, just a transparent cover of angst, and here, at a funeral viewing, he was wearing a ball cap that said *Mother Fucker Legend.*

Steve had a joke on the tip of his tongue, but life had seriously reduced the list of things he could joke about; life had put a face on every failing, vice, or disease that could, in his callow youth, be amusing. So instead he said, "Surprised he is here."

"Who knows?" Les shrugged. "There were lots like him."

"Yeah?"

"Yeah."

"First person I knew who had a nervous breakdown," continued Steve. "I didn't even know what that meant, just that he couldn't come to school, and Bugsy picked up his assignments, and then that stopped. I heard a story but—"

Les shrugged, and Steve went quiet.

Every year, for almost as long as Steve remembered, the town—a remarkably unathletic town, a town of potlucks and obsessive lawn mowers—had held a road race, and after a while it became important. With a cash prize, T-shirts, and press. Steve remembered that there was a local boy named Jason who could run better than anyone he had ever seen; when he ran he made Steve question his own definition of running. He saw Jason on the roads at 5 a.m. and he saw Jason at 6 p.m. followed by his dad; Jason, like Steve Fonyo and Leon Spinks, was chasing a dream. One year, the town invited a Kenyan distance runner to its race. And the do-gooders picked him up at the airport. They went on CBC—*It's our Maritime hospitality*—they served him his first lobster, and, of course, he won. And of course, he was wearing a singlet emblazoned with the town's crest. And, of course, he put two and a half minutes between himself and Jason and it made the town happy to see Jason put in his place. And you would have had to stand them all in front of their Maker—with the keys to Heaven in His hand—before they would admit their happiness, even to themselves.

*

Steve watched Nick shuffle to the beet chips and stand there, immobile. He saw one of Mister Logan's elderly cousins stumble over in her belted dress and ask, "Who are you?"

"Do you think so many are here because of how it happened?" he finally asked.

"Sure," conceded Les.

"One shot to the head?"

Les shrugged noncommittally.

"Do they know anything?"

Les shrugged his cop shrug again.

"In his car, right?"

Len shrugged *maybe*.

"Why would anyone bother to off him? He was eighty."

"That's not the way it works."

Steve remembered that Mister Logan smelled like salt cod and he had white spittle on the corners of his mouth. He stuttered when he got excited—like when he came into the locker room to make sure no one was smoking, or when you got sent to his office by the hall monitors, or when he interrupted math class to collect *The Mikado* lead—and you weren't supposed to notice any of that, but you did. And when you are young, you know things and you *think* you know things, and sometimes you don't know which is which, and there was nothing you could do anyway. Was there? Mister Logan was one of those people who mattered.

"Seems fair to me," Steve blurted. "Seems fair after everything—"

"Well, Steve," said Les, sounding like a man who had been on the job his entire life, a man who had been on too many stakeouts. "Fairness is not a real thing like gravel. Or beer. Fairness is something you imagine in the same way that you once imagined that Trudy would ask you to the Twerp Week dance."

Steve smiled despite himself.

"I forgot you were a funny guy, Les."

whirrrrrr whirrrr whirrrr rat a tat tat

Steve looked at the door where the janitor had been standing. Above it was an illuminated red-and-white *EXIT* sign inside a steel cage. Next to a banner that said *Panther Pride*. Behind the *EXIT* sign, Les had installed the video surveillance camera that would record Steve and any suspicious parties as they left, but Steve didn't know that.

If he started walking now, he could get to the street before he felt too tired, he told himself. *Think positive thoughts.*

Gábor

They were an unlikely pair of travellers: a slight middle-aged man and an elderly woman in a paisley cape. She had the air of someone who expected to be seated in the front row of funerals and weddings, no matter how tenuous her connection might be. He had an uneasy sniff.

They sat with their backs to their boarding gate, and unlike the novice flyers—the naïfs with cardboard boxes and hard-sided Samsonite luggage, economy tickets to Deer Lake, NL,—they did not seem worried about missing anything. They seemed offhand.

Her day had started in Winnipeg, his in Toronto, where they now sat waiting. Her stillness felt like a statement, his a compromise. Across the tile airport floor in an unyielding plastic chair was a young Japanese traveller engrossed in an iPad, next to him a tanned woman in Gucci flowered sneakers and a coral cardigan.

And then, the man—his name was Vikram— began to talk rapidly, as though an idea had just come to him, an idea that he had to share before the details were lost like someone's overbooked seat.

"Do you know that Ottawa gives medals to bureaucrats who devise ways of deceiving the public?" As though it had been on the news. The woman—her name was Katarina—did not turn to face him. "Yes Men," he added, as she stared straight ahead, as though his voice was coming in on the public-address system.

"They fly them to Ottawa and they put them up in a grand hotel and they take their picture with the Governor General, and they aren't even like Goebbels who did, at least, believe in a cause. A cause so terrible that he killed, when the end was near, all of his little children, including Heidrun, who was only four, and Helmut, the only boy, who wore braces. He killed them all in the *Vorbunker.* The Yes Men don't believe in anything."

"Goebbels is such a tired trope," Katarina replied without the bother of emotion.

"Well—" Vikram tried to defend himself.

"I am surprised you did not mention he had a PhD in literature."

"Who doesn't?" he snapped back too quickly.

"I know you have your issues with academia because of Margaret and all of that, and I understand, but not *everyone* has a PhD."

"Point taken."

"It took cousin Deidre six years to complete hers, with all that trouble with her dissertation and that little man who was obsessed with the Chinese long zither."

"I recall."

"Why do you know so much about the Goebbels children?"

"We all have our interests—"

Katarina touched the collar of her cape, signalling the

end of the conversation. At that moment, the traveller with the iPad stood up, cradling a white stuffed bear in the crook of his arm. Vikram watched the man float into a gift shop, his feet as light as a palm court piano trio; he watched the bear float with him. The stranger's backpack was strung with smaller animals—a lion, a bearded goat—and Vikram stared, trying to decipher their meaning.

Five minutes later, Vikram and Katarina picked up their carry-ons and shuffled to the boarding gate, the bear man paces behind them. The stranger was dressed all in black with high-top running shoes with gold crown-shaped fasteners that never touched the ground. His hair fashionably undercut. Awaiting them was an Air Canada flight operated by Lufthansa.

"You mustn't get yourself upset," Katarina said as they showed their passes.

"You are right."

Vikram had fine correct features and thick dark hair, but he could not, it seemed, bring himself to parade his looks. Something made him hide them, to bury them under an expression of vagueness and worry. He could have been handsome if he had tried; he could have been the kind of man you would turn your head to look at, but he wasn't.

"Do you have your pills?" Katarina asked.

"Yes."

"We are going to have a lovely trip."

"Yes, we are."

"Did I tell you how happy I am that you could come with me?"

"Yes."

Silence. And then a sniff.

"We should walk a lot," Vikram declared. "Whenever I go abroad that is what I do, I walk."

"I don't care for museums."

*

Minutes into the ten-hour flight, the attendant gave Katarina a blanket, which she wrapped around herself like a woman her age might. That age where she needed people for things she didn't want to need them for.

The attendant had a German accent and wore frameless eyeglasses and a signet ring, none of which Katarina particularly noticed. He was the kind of man who *did* parade his good looks; other passengers could imagine him skiing at Zugspitze above the clouds.

Katarina had the window seat, Vikram, the aisle. Like an undercover air marshal, he kept his leather shoulder bag tucked to his side.

Across the aisle, the stranger with the iPad was holding the bear upright in his lap. And then the bear whispered, low enough so that only Vikram could hear: "You are right, you know, about the Yes Men—they don't believe in anything."

Ah ha! Vikram thought.

"They are an oleaginous lot," the bear continued, "they should all burn in hell."

Vikram met the bear's black eyes and nodded *thanks. Ah ha.* Not everything was upside down, not everyone was part of the problem. Relieved, Vikram smiled at Katarina as though the awkward outburst over the Yes Men had never happened, as though the bear had not just taken his side, and it felt good to have something that was just his, a secret he could hold inside like a daydream.

Silence. And then a sniff.

"It is rare for me to travel without my instruments," Vikram confessed.

"Yes," conceded Katarina, "you usually have an advantage. You bring your viola with you when you perform. I never know what will be there. Once I arrived, and they had a Yamaha piano and they had painted it white."

She allowed herself a chuckle, and the joke amused Vikram, or so he would have her think.

"Is your own a Steinway?"

"Of course. Freda has a Roland, which plays other instruments." She snorted a mild laugh that did not require her to smile. "They played the cello part on it for Rutger, who didn't see the humour. Cellists can be so dour."

"Ha ha." Barely a laugh.

"It was wonderful the foundation got us these tickets," Katarina declared. "These conferences always have interesting exhibits and you see so many people."

"How long has it been for you?"

"Thirty years. The last time I was in Budapest, the State Opera House was being redone."

Silence.

"They believe that the mother Magda killed the children," Vikram announced abruptly, startling Katarina. "Not Goebbels. She had a dentist give them morphine. There were chances to save them, to take them away before the Russians arrived, but she refused, and when they found the children they were in nightclothes and the girls had ribbons in their hair."

"You must stop with Goebbels! It makes you sound dim."

Stung, Vikram looked at the bear, who rolled his eyes, and whispered, "Nobody wants to hear what *she* thinks! The vain old bat should just be happy you are here! She should be happy someone does not punch her in the face."

Vikram nodded. He wanted to tell the bear about his home phone, which was one of the reasons he had gone on this trip. The phone had call waiting. If he was on a call, one he did not wish to interrupt, his phone would *beep beep beep* if someone else was trying to reach him. This was problematic because of his ex-wife. If he did not answer, Margaret would call again. And again. One day he was on an important call, and his ex-wife phoned eight times—*beep beep beep*—and by the time the call was over, his anxiety was so high that he fainted. Now she could ring all she wanted, she could just ring ring ring.

The attendant served Katarina and Vikram salmon on cabbage, along with two kinds of cheese, and a warm bun with butter. Vanilla ice cream for dessert. Katarina requested a second glass of red wine, which the attendant, whose name was Manfred, promptly delivered.

"How is your new CD?" Vikram asked while waiting for the trays to be cleared.

"Coming out soon. The engineer is very good; he worked at CBC."

"With Gould?"

"Oh yes. And all that that entails. The humming, the singing. Very difficult."

"But you are happy with it?"

"Well, yes. I do some Gershwin; I do all the arrangements. This will probably be my last."

"Why?"

"I am not the same as I was at thirty. I am more interested in writing. Historical fiction. I have friends who write, and that is what I will probably do. Cousin Boyd writes beautifully. His son just graduated from medical school. Very talented that family."

"Is that Royce?"

"Yes."

"Royce who went to the Caribbean?"

"Yes," Katarina confirmed.

And across the aisle, the bear burst out laughing: "Oh yes, *everyone* who graduates from Last Chance Med School is very talented. It is on a volcanic island, for fuck's sake. What kind of quack graduates from a med school on a ghastly Dutch island with one gas station, one road, and a volcano?"

And Vikram said, "I see."

"Do you see the children at all?" Katarina asked after another nap and a bite of the chocolate Manfred had delivered. She had an opal ring on her right hand, and from time to time, she held it out to admire it. When she was young and striking, she had tossed on her jewellery carelessly, more important things on her mind. Who might be in love with her. Who was under her spell. Who she might cruelly abandon.

"No."

"I see."

"She tells them that she met him six months after she left me. She tells them I am a poor musician, and he is a hero who got a medal for his work on those crooked drug trials. The ones involving the deformed children."

"Is that why you dislike the Yes Men? Because of him?"

"Yes."

"Well you should just say so. Just say what you mean."

Silence.

"This Thanksgiving, we will have a party," Katarina announced, foregoing further discussion. "I know you usually have plans but we can all play, and it will be grand. Let's plan for *that*. Maybe cousin Deidre can come; she is seeing that woman who teaches Balinese drumming, and that could be fun. Let's plan for a party and everyone will play."

Vikram sniffed, and Katarina resumed her questioning.

"Did you get any money from the house?"

"No."

"Why did you let her take it?"

"Because that is just the type of person I am. I just take what I need."

"Well, your mother was the same way. She could do a lot with very little. She could find ways to take trips and she would make all of her own dresses."

"She always spoke highly of you."

"I was sorry when she moved East. She had a talent like you. Despite all of her troubles, she had a talent."

"Thank you."

Silence.

Manfred arrived to deliver hot towels, which he held in a pair of tongs.

"A mobster in New Jersey had a near-death experience and he spent two minutes in Hell," Vikram stated the moment that Manfred was gone. "And it was a terrible Hell: there was intense heat and a horrible screeching noise—the sound of bare metal on metal. And there was a screen and it showed the faces of all of the innocent people he had wronged. And who do you think the Devil was surrounded by?"

"I don't know."

"Government Yes Men."

"I see."

"And afterwards the mobster changed his ways."

"Ah."

"And then a little boy was pulled from a swimming pool and he went to Heaven, and there were only toys and ponies there. And there were no corrupt mandarins. Not a single one!"

The bear nodded, and when he did, Vikram sensed an evil in his eyes, a malevolence, that he liked.

"When we arrive in Budapest, Myriam will make us a lovely lunch," declared Katarina. "She is so good like that. She doesn't even have a stove or a microwave and she does such a wonderful job. She will make us a lunch."

Vikram closed his eyes, and he wrestled with the question he had been wrestling with for months: How big does your action have to be before it overwrites everything in your life? What does it take? Let's say you have a good job; you volunteer with sick children. Do you have to suffocate your elderly mother in her sleep for *that t*o define you, or is it enough to get drunk at her funeral and run over someone's dog? Do you have to steal drugs from a pharmacy to become a one-dimensional bad person? Or is a second breakdown enough? He looked at the bear for an answer, but the bear had turned his head to face the window.

"There is a woman I am interested in." Vikram surprised Katarina, making the confession suddenly.

"Tell me about her."

"She is very kind, she is cultured; we share some of the same philosophies in life, but she is a widow and she is older."

"How much older?"

"Fourteen years."

"You are probably too young for that."

Vikram shrugged, deflated.

"My cousin Charles and his wife have been married for forty years and they spend all of their time together," said Katrina, her voice sharp with disdain. "I could not live like that. If I want to have lunch with a friend, I can. If I want to go to a show alone, I will. Charles's wife, Gudrun, has, for thirty years, called herself a painter. She has no talent, no ability to create anything relevant or haunting. It is just *schlock* that must be justified in extravagant overwritten notes."

Vikram knew Charles, a conductor. He shrugged, not willing to indict Charles just yet.

"A bit like Margaret, I dare say, and her forays into literature."

"Thank you," Vikram replied.

"And when one partner dies, it is quite tragic."

Katarina stared into space, as though she was willing this tragic end: Charles reduced to a sobbing scrap of nothing, his talentless wife buried after forty years of shared breakfasts and evening walks, words that did not even have to be spoken.

"I have reached that point when I no longer enjoy human tragedy," Katarina loftily announced, and Vikram did not believe her.

Katarina didn't know that Vikram was at a crossroads any more than she knew what Charles really felt. Vikram was deciding what was fixable in his life and what was not. He was compiling a mental spreadsheet with plus and minus columns, as intricate as a Bartók concerto.

"Ask her about Gábor," the bear piped up, "Don't let the old bat sell you a bill of goods."

Everyone knew that Gábor and Katarina had once been a couple, at one point, as dramatic as a thunderstorm. And afterwards, there was that terrible business of Gábor and the psych ward and talk that he might never play again. Gábor with a talent that rare and dangerous, listening to one opera over and over again. Abandoned.

Vikram gave the bear a nod that said, *Okay*.

The plane landed at an airport renamed for Franz Liszt, the piano virtuoso and composer, Liszt whose playing was so passionate that he was said to destroy fragile instruments, and could only, according to Bösendorfer, be served by their grand pianos. Passengers were racing by: a couple carrying backpacks, a hippy. A man wearing a black bomber jacket that said Pain is Past Pleasure over his heart hugged the man with the malevolent bear. The greeter was holding another bear that could have been its twin. The two men put the bears face to face—to kiss—and Vikram turned away.

The new pills were helping, Vikram decided as he sniffed the air. He could see things that he couldn't see before. Good people, bad people. Options and outcomes. He could see where all of this was inevitably going. He could see Gábor, old and broken, as clearly as he could see his own face in a bathroom mirror.

He and Katarina kept walking.

"Does Charles still hear from Gábor?" he asked, gently at first. "They were inseparable."

"Oh, I don't know." She bristled.

"Did Charles tell Gábor you are coming to Budapest?"

Katarina ignored him.

"Did he?" Vikram repeated the question.

"Oh, I don't know." Katarina bristled again, and stared, in an attempt to distract Vikram, at the distance; she stared as though she was on an artfully lit stage in an auburn wig and drawn-on brows, commanding an entire audience to be silent. She stared as though the whole world was watching.

"You are starting to sound like a Yes Man."

She was so startled by the boldness in his voice that she picked up her stride. "Oh, look! There is someone with a sign for us. I knew they would come. Look, someone is waiting!"

And then she glanced behind her, and Vikram was gone.

Acknowledgements

I am delighted that this book is being published by Goose Lane Editions, which year after year produces beautiful books that are profound and rich and meaningful. Thanks to Goose Lane and Susanne Alexander for seeing the joy and the sorrow in this collection. It was a privilege to again work with Bethany Gibson, Goose Lane's immensely gifted fiction editor, who approached this project with an artist's vision yet held it accountable when it needed to be brought back to earth. It is because of Bethany that these stories are the best they can be. I am grateful for her rare talent and her unyielding professionalism. This book also benefitted from the superb copy-editing of Paula Sarson, who fixed my mistakes and reminded me of rules I had forgotten.

When researching this book, I received location notes from my son, Paddy, who once worked in curious places, and feedback from my daughter, Hannah. My husband, Andrew Vaughan, drove me across Nova Scotia so that I could collect my own notes. In this book, as in others, I write about the things that can — if left on their own — break us, hoping to strip them of that power. I use humour to heal, a device that I have counted on during challenging times in my life, and it is my hope that readers, faced with their own inevitable struggles, take something from this.

Some of these stories appeared in literary journals: the *Antigonish Review*, the *Danforth Review*, the *Nashwaak Review*, and the *Offbeat*. My thanks to them.

I am most grateful to Arts Nova Scotia and the Canada Council for the Arts for the generous support that made this book possible.

Elaine McCluskey writes about bouncers and boxers, the aggrieved and the unlucky. She has been described as a "vigorous, colourful and often humorous writer, with a sharp and sometimes wicked eye" (*Globe and Mail*). A former Atlantic Canada bureau chief with The Canadian Press, McCluskey has also worked as a book editor, a writing coach, and a journalism instructor at the University of King's College.

Rafael Has Pretty Eyes is McCluskey's sixth book of fiction. Her previous publications include *The Watermelon Social*, a finalist for the John and Margaret Savage First Book Award; *The Most Heartless Town in Canada*; and *Going Fast*, winner of the H.R. (Bill) Percy Award. McCluskey's stories have won the Other Voices short story contest, and been chosen as finalists for the Journey Prize and the Fish Short Story Prize in Ireland. They have also appeared in numerous anthologies and journals, including *Room*, the *Antigonish Review*, and the *Fiddlehead*. McCluskey lives in Dartmouth, Nova Scotia.

Photo: Andrew Vaughan